"I'm so scared, Rex. What if he hurts my baby?"

"I'll tear him apart." Brave words.

But it was what Nadia needed to hear. She reached up and touched his face. "Thank you."

He moved into her light caress, craving her touch. And before he knew what was happening, their lips met. Fueled by tension and pent-up feelings, the kiss was not gentle, but Rex didn't think Nadia wanted gentle. She battled as fiercely as he did. Her hands touched him everywhere, while his got caught in that wonderful cloud of hair.

Rex didn't know how the kiss had started, or how he'd let it get so out of hand. With Nadia invading his senses, every sane thought flew from his brain. The only thing he did know was that he never wanted it to end.

But it had to end. "Nadia…" he murmured against her mouth.

"Please don't let go of me. If you stop touching me, the fear will crush me."

Dear Harlequin Intrigue Reader,

It might be warm outside, but our June lineup will thrill and chill you!

* This month, we have a couple of great miniseries. *Man of Her Dreams* is the spine-tingling conclusion to Debra Webb's trilogy THE ENFORCERS. And there are just two installments left in B.J. Daniels's McCALLS' MONTANA series—*High-Caliber Cowboy* is out now, and *Shotgun Surrender* will be available next month.

* We also have two fantastic special promotions. First, is our Gothic ECLIPSE title, *Mystique*, by Charlotte Douglas. And Dani Sinclair brings you *D.B. Hayes, Detective*, the second installment in our LIPSTICK LTD. promotion featuring sexy sleuths.

* Last, but definitely not least, is Jessica Andersen's *The Sheriff's Daughter*. Sparks fly between a medical investigator and a vet in this exciting medical thriller.

* Also, keep your eyes peeled for Joanna Wayne's THE GENTLEMAN'S CLUB, available from Signature Spotlight.

This month, and every month, we promise to deliver six of the best romantic suspense titles around. Don't miss a single one!

Sincerely,

Denise O'Sullivan
Senior Editor
Harlequin Intrigue

BOUNTY HUNTER HONOR

KARA LENNOX

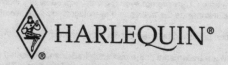

TORONTO • NEW YORK • LONDON
AMSTERDAM • PARIS • SYDNEY • HAMBURG
STOCKHOLM • ATHENS • TOKYO • MILAN • MADRID
PRAGUE • WARSAW • BUDAPEST • AUCKLAND

ISBN 0-373-22853-8

BOUNTY HUNTER HONOR

Copyright © 2005 by Karen Leabo

ABOUT THE AUTHOR

Texas native Kara Lennox has been an art director, typesetter, textbook editor and reporter. She's worked in a boutique, a health club and an ad agency. She's been an antiques dealer and even a blackjack dealer. But no work has made her happier than writing romance novels.

When not writing, Kara indulges in an ever-changing array of weird hobbies. (Her latest passions are treasure hunting and creating mosaics.) She loves to hear from readers. You can visit her Web site and drop her a note at www.karalennox.com.

Books by Kara Lennox

HARLEQUIN INTRIGUE
756—BOUNTY HUNTER RANSOM†
805—BOUNTY HUNTER REDEMPTION†
853—BOUNTY HUNTER HONOR†

HARLEQUIN AMERICAN ROMANCE
840—VIRGIN PROMISE
856—TWIN EXPECTATIONS
871—TAME AN OLDER MAN
893—BABY BY THE BOOK
917—THE UNLAWFULLY WEDDED PRINCESS
934—VIXEN IN DISGUISE*
942—PLAIN JANE'S PLAN*
951—SASSY CINDERELLA*
974—FORTUNE'S TWINS
990—THE MILLIONAIRE NEXT DOOR
1052—THE FORGOTTEN COWBOY
1068—HOMETOWN HONEY††

†Code of the Cobra
*How To Marry a Hardison
†† Blond Justice

CAST OF CHARACTERS

Rex Bettencourt—One of the country's top bounty hunters. But the ex-marine sniper has a terrible secret he's never confessed to anyone—a secret that could potentially get someone killed.

Nadia Penn—Granddaughter of a KGB defector, research scientist and inventor of the Petro-Nano, an exciting technology that could solve the world's energy problems—or cause instantaneous global meltdown.

Lily Penn—Nadia's two-year-old daughter, kidnapped from her stroller right under Nadia's nose.

Peter Danilov—Nadia's Russian ex-husband. Handsome, charismatic and very dangerous. He has Lily, and there is only one way Nadia can get her back—turn over the Petro-Nano.

Denise Petrovski, alias "Rat Face"—Peter's Russian girlfriend. She is blindly loyal to her mother country and crazily in love with Peter. But could she harm an innocent child?

Detective Lyle Palmer—A cop whose incompetence is exceeded only by his ambition—and his resentment of the First Strike Agency bounty hunters.

Detective Craig Cartwright—The only cop any of the bounty hunters trust.

Lori Bettencourt—Rex's sister and fellow bounty hunter, more clever and capable than anyone gives her credit for.

Prologue

Something was wrong. The certainty started as a prickling of unease at the back of Nadia's neck. But it grew until it twisted in her gut. She glanced first over one shoulder, then the other. Nothing. Nobody.

Then she looked down at the stroller, where her two-year-old daughter had been sleeping soundly while Nadia shopped for baby clothes.

The stroller was empty.

At first, she tamped down her panic and tried to find some logical explanation for Lily's absence. Had another shopper at the mall found the baby irresistible and picked her up for a quick cuddle? Had Lily, getting more clever with her hands by the day, unfastened her safety strap and crawled out of the stroller herself?

But a quick scan in all directions at the baby store produced no sign of Lily. Around Nadia, other women calmly sifted through tiny, pastel-hued dresses and booties, chatting among themselves. No one sensed the terrible rent in the fabric of Nadia's reality. But her baby was gone, vanished like a mist.

Abandoning the stroller, Nadia ran out into the mall,

looking frantically for her child. Nothing. Everything looked deceptively calm, sickeningly normal. No sinister persons were hurrying off with Lily in their arms.

The panic she'd kept at bay rose again in her chest, in her throat, a scream of horror threatening. *No,* she told herself sternly, she would not panic. Panic would not make Lily reappear. She would tell a store employee, who would make an announcement and contact security.

A gloved hand around her arm stopped her as she was about to carry out her plan. She turned to find a blond woman with sharp, rodentlike features gazing malevolently at her. The woman was well turned out, in slim black pants and a fitted silk blouse, her hair expertly cut and highlighted, but nothing could have made her pretty given the sneer on her face.

"Not a sound," she said softly, her voice carrying the trace of cigarettes and a Russian accent. "If you ever want to see your daughter again, you won't raise an alarm, you won't call the police, you won't tell anyone. Do you understand?"

Frozen inside, all Nadia could do was nod. "Is this Peter's doing?" But she already knew. After her divorce, she'd spent months watching her rearview mirror, screening phone calls, checking the locks on windows and doors. All that time, there'd been no word from her ex-husband. Just within the past couple of weeks, she'd finally begun to feel safe.

She'd been a fool.

The blond woman didn't answer her question. Instead she handed Nadia a folded piece of paper. "The nonnegotiable terms for Lily's safe return are here. Follow them to the letter and your daughter will not be harmed."

Nadia accepted the paper, her hands numb, her whole body turned to cold lead. This wasn't happening. This could not be happening. She should grab this woman, scream for help. But even as the woman strode confidently away, out of the store and into the mall where she quickly blended in with the crowd, Nadia remained mute, fears for her daughter's safety paralyzing her.

She opened the folded paper, though she was already pretty sure what the terms would be. She had access to something Peter wanted very badly, and it wasn't his daughter.

Chapter One

A fugitive with millions of dollars and a group of loyal and capable bodyguards wasn't the easiest criminal to catch. But the price on Jethro Banner's head—fifty thousand dollars—was enough to make more than one bounty hunter try.

Most quickly abandoned the quest. But Rex Bettencourt was not the type to give up easily. As a sniper for the Marines' Maritime Special Purpose Force, he'd learned all he needed to know about patience. He'd once lain on his belly covered with camouflage for two days without food or water, sweating in the intense, steamy heat, letting fist-size bugs crawl over his body without a twitch as he waited for a target to emerge from his secret bunker. Compared to that terrorist warlord, Jethro Banner was a cakewalk.

Sheer doggedness and some hefty bribes in the right circles had yielded Jethro's location, in a heavily fortified mansion near San Antonio, Texas. A week of surveillance, waiting for an opportunity to take down Jethro when he was alone and vulnerable, was about to pay off. The freelance bomber had broken his molar on a macadamia nut—according to the pool boy on Rex's pay-roll—necessitating an emergency trip to the dentist.

Jethro's bodyguards could not possibly make the dentist's office totally secure on short notice.

What was even better, Rex had gotten to Jethro's dentist and persuaded him to inject his patient with a mild tranquilizer, ensuring he would be easy to apprehend.

By the time the fugitive arrived, whining like a six-year-old about the pain, Rex was already waiting in the exam room next door to Jethro's, wearing a mask and scrubs in case anyone checked. Jethro didn't question the hypodermic the dentist shot into his mouth—he cared only for his comfort. Within a couple of minutes he was feeling no pain and had a dopey grin on his face, every muscle in his body relaxed.

Rex slipped into the room with Jethro. "I'll take it from here," he whispered to the dentist, who nodded. He and his receptionist—the only employee who hadn't already evacuated—left through the back door.

"Open your mouth, please," Rex said in what he hoped was a soothing voice. Jethro did as asked, utterly compliant. Rex stuffed cotton into the fugitive's mouth—enough to muffle his cries of panic when he realized what was going on. His bodyguards were only a few feet away, in the waiting room.

When Jethro resembled a hamster with its cheeks packed with seeds, Rex lifted the armrest on the dentist's chair and in one swift move pushed the man forward and bent his right arm behind him. "Make a sound and I'll tear out your shoulder," Rex said calmly as he captured Jethro's other arm and cuffed him. There was no resistance and not a peep from the formerly formidable fugitive. Man, whatever the dentist had given him, it had worked.

Rex hauled Jethro to his feet. The man stood precariously for a moment, then toppled like a child's pile of blocks. Rex caught him before he could hit the floor. "Jethro?"

Easing him down, Rex pulled some of the cotton out of Jethro's mouth, not wanting to suffocate an unconscious man. Jethro smiled. "Where we goin', Mama?"

"We're goin' for a ride," Rex answered in a falsetto. "Then some nice FBI agents are going to put you in prison, where you'll get to be the girlfriend of some guy named Bubba."

"Okay."

Rex saw no way around it—he would have to carry the bulky Jethro Banner out of the dentist's office. The fugitive wasn't going anywhere under his own steam. He only hoped Lori had brought the Blazer around to the back door as he'd told her to do. His little sister was smart and tough—for a girl—but she was green as a mountain meadow when it came to bounty hunting. He'd only brought her along on this job because at least he could keep an eye on her when she was working with him.

With a sigh he heaved Jethro—who was not a small man—over his shoulder and headed for the storage room, which had a door leading directly to the parking lot.

When he opened the door to the storage room, he stopped cold. Two muscle-bound gorillas stood waiting for him; one of them held a .44 pointed at Rex's head.

"Going somewhere?" the gorilla with the gun asked.

Hell. Jethro's bodyguards must have gotten tipped off somehow. Rex dumped Jethro onto the carpet. He could have ducked back into the hallway and drawn his Glock from the holster at the small of his back… His gut twisted at the prospect. He was pretty sure the bodyguard wouldn't shoot him, he reasoned. A messy murder would only draw unwanted attention to him and his boss, and his prime directive would be to protect Jethro.

"Get Mr. Banner," the gunman instructed his friend. Gorilla No. 2 stepped over to his inert boss and tried to coax him to his feet, but it was no use. Jethro was barely conscious.

"I can't carry him by myself," the bodyguard whined.

"Drag him, then," the gunman said sharply. "Unless you want to go back to prison."

This seemed to motivate the second man. He grasped Jethro under the arms and dragged him toward the door. The gunman, his weapon still trained on Rex, opened the door. He'd only gotten it open a couple of inches when it slammed the rest of the way with the force of a cannon shot. In an instinctive move, Rex dived for the floor.

The door hit the gunman square in the face. Lori burst in, deflected his weapon, then did something so fast with her hands that they blurred. The gunman's weapon flew through the air and landed on a pile of cardboard boxes.

Before the gunman even knew what hit him, Lori had swept one of his feet out from under him. He fell facedown on the floor.

Rex didn't waste too much time watching his sister

in action. He went for Gorilla No. 2, who was so shocked by Lori's entrance that he didn't even make a move for his own weapon. Rex came at him full speed, knocking him in the chin with the heel of his hand and snapping his head back. The bodyguard dropped Jethro—who didn't seem to mind—and stumbled back against a set of shelves. A small box that apparently contained something heavy fell on the goon's head, stunning him further. Then it was a simple matter for Rex to drag him to the ground and secure his wrists behind him. Thank God he'd thought to bring some zip ties, just in case.

He turned to help Lori but found she already had the first bodyguard neatly hog-tied.

"You were supposed to stay in the car," Rex growled.

"You're welcome," she said sweetly. "Think these other two are wanted for anything? If so, this one's mine." She nudged her takedown with her foot.

BACK IN PAYTON, TEXAS, Rex sat behind his desk at the First Strike Agency, plowing through neglected paperwork like an Uzi through balsa wood. He hated paperwork, but it was a necessary evil. He sustained himself through the tedium by picturing himself on a beach in Tahiti, sipping a mai tai, a bikini-clad woman smoothing suntan lotion on his shoulders as he listened to the soothing sound of the surf.

He'd already made the reservations. As soon as he finished here, he was heading to the airport for a long, long overdue vacation. With the reward money from recovering Jethro Banner, he could afford to do it up first-class.

He became so engrossed in one particular mental picture that he closed his eyes to more fully enjoy it. It was only when he opened his eyes again that he realized he was no longer alone in the office. A petite brunette stood in front of his desk, an expectant look on her pixie face.

Images of the bikini woman vanished as reality intruded—although he had to say, in this case, it wasn't a bad trade-off. The woman staring at him with beseeching dark eyes was small and slender, with a mop of dark curls cascading in defiant disarray around her head and shoulders. Her huge green eyes, topped with dramatically straight, dark brows, were her best feature, but her straight nose and full, pink lips all contributed to a face that was an odd mixture of boldness, intelligence and an undeniable frailty.

She'd probably look okay in a bikini, too.

Unfortunately, he couldn't miss the terror that lay just beneath the surface of her demeanor, which could mean one of two things, or possibly both: abusive husband-boyfriend, or missing child.

He was not in any shape to take on either of those types of cases right now. One, they didn't pay enough. Two, in about five minutes he was officially on vacation.

But, damn it, he was the only one at the First Strike office. Everybody else was out working cases, even Lori.

"I'm looking for Rex Bettencourt," she said, her voice soft, sure, but not without a tiny tremor.

It figured she'd be looking for him. He considered denying all knowledge of any Rex Bettencourt, but he couldn't turn his back on a woman in trouble. Never had been able to. "That would be me."

"I read about you in that magazine. They say you're the best."

"I am the best," he confirmed, not out of any need for an ego trip, but because it was true. In the four years since he'd come to work for First Strike, the agency co-founded by his father and his father's army buddy, Ace McCullough, he'd amassed more reward money than any other bounty hunter in the country. Mostly he managed to do it working in conjunction with law enforcement, so police and federal agents not only welcomed him, but sought him out on tough cases. His success sometimes afforded him unwanted publicity.

"My daughter has been taken."

Score one for Rex's instincts. "By her father?"

The woman nodded.

"Why don't you let me refer you to one of my—"

"No. I want you. You're the best."

"The best doesn't come cheap," Rex said. Though the First Strike office was his home base, Rex was an independent contractor. Ace, sole owner of First Strike since the death of Rex's father almost two years ago, let all the bounty hunters charge what they wanted and pursue the cases that interested them, paying a small percentage to the agency in return for an office and administrative support. So long as each brought in a certain minimum—and Rex always far exceeded the minimum—they could handle the job any way they chose.

"I'm prepared to pay whatever it takes," the woman said.

"I charge five hundred dollars a day plus expenses." He figured that would scare her off.

She didn't even blink. "It's not a problem. Just get my daughter back."

Rex sighed. He couldn't say no. The case sounded routine enough. Maybe he could wrap it up in a day or two. He got up, dragged over a chair from a neighboring desk and situated it next to his, rather than on the other side of the desk. He didn't want any barriers, physical or emotional, between him and his potential client. If he took on her case, they would have to trust each other completely. He refused to work any other way.

She sat down, clutching her brown leather purse in her lap so tightly her knuckles turned white.

Rex picked up a pen and a legal pad. "Your name?"

"Nadia Penn."

"Tell me what's going on, Nadia. After I hear your story, I'll decide whether I can help you. Do you have legal custody of the child?"

"Yes."

"And the child's father?"

"My ex-husband. He gave up all parental rights when we divorced six months ago."

That admission gave Rex pause. What kind of man gave up all rights to his children?

"He was abusive," she said without hesitating a beat. "He sent me to the hospital with a broken jaw. No court was going to give him custody, and he didn't want to pay me child support."

The thought of any man using his fists on such a delicate, defenseless creature made Rex's gut churn. It was that sliver of compassion he felt for the fairer sex that had ruined him, ended his military career.

"Legal rights aside, has he had contact with his daughter prior to this?" Rex asked. "Have you allowed him to visit?"

"Peter Danilov has no personal interest in Lily. He cares nothing about her. He took her to blackmail me. I have access to something he wants very badly, and he intends to barter for it with my child's life."

Good Lord. So much for the simple, straightforward case he'd envisioned. "So, whatever it is, give it to him. Nothing is worth a child's life."

"It isn't that easy."

He sighed. "This sounds like a matter for the police."

"Do you know how many children are kidnapped by noncustodial parents? And do you know how little the police care? Anyway, I couldn't risk it." Nadia opened her purse and pulled out a plain white sheet of paper, folded. She handed it to him.

He took the paper gingerly by one corner. Ah, hell, why bother? She'd probably already destroyed any potential forensic evidence.

"You can touch it," she said. "It's already been analyzed. No prints but mine. Common photocopy paper, Canon Inkjet ink. Nontraceable."

"I thought you didn't go to the police."

"I didn't. I work in a research lab. I did the analysis myself."

"Ah." He tried not to show his surprise. He wouldn't have pegged this delicate, fairylike creature as a hard-nosed scientist, though he ought to know by now not to let anyone's outward appearance surprise him. His last stint in Korea should have burned that message into his brain once and for all.

He read the note, which set forth the terms she would have to meet if she wanted to see her daughter alive again. She would be required to deliver a package to a certain place at a certain time, then leave. The package would be picked up, the contents verified. Only then would the child be released at an undisclosed location. She would be notified after the fact.

If she agreed to these terms, she was to go today at 3:00 p.m. to the Forest Ridge Mall food court wearing a red shirt and wait at least fifteen minutes, after which she would be contacted as to where and when to make the drop.

Peter Danilov obviously liked cloak-and-dagger games. Such an affinity for drama could be used against him.

Rex asked Nadia the obvious. "What does Peter want from you?" The note simply referred to a "package," which Rex assumed meant Nadia knew what it was.

"I can't tell you that."

"And I can't win this game playing with only half a deck."

"I can't tell you without breaching the security of the United States," she said quietly. "But suffice it to say, it's something very dangerous. I could never put it into Peter's hands. Which is why I need you to get my baby back."

National security? Dangerous?

"Whoa, wait a minute. You don't by any chance work for—"

"JanCo Labs."

Ah, hell. JanCo Labs was a huge facility tucked away in the piney woods of East Texas a few miles from Payton. The lab worked almost exclusively on top secret government contracts—everything from gene splicing to weapons technology.

Rex was intrigued despite himself.

"Do you have any way to contact Peter?"

"No."

"Do you have any idea where he might have taken your daughter?"

"No, I'm sorry. I've had no contact with him for months."

"Do you believe he will actually harm Lily?"

She hesitated. "He never physically hurt her before. But I do know one thing. If he suspects even for a moment that I've come to you or anyone for help, he will spirit Lily off to Russia with him, and I will never see her again."

NADIA ENDURED the next hour of tedious questions solely because she knew Rex Bettencourt was her only hope.

She hadn't been too sure when she'd first walked up to the First Strike Agency. She'd read of his impressive success rate in a national magazine and had considered it an extremely lucky break that the bounty hunter was based in her own backyard. But when she'd seen his place of business, with its faded, tattered awning and grimy windows, she'd been less than impressed. First Strike was in a bad area of town to begin with, sandwiched between a bail bondsman and a pawnshop. But even if the neighborhood hadn't discouraged her, the office itself would have.

Narrow and deep, the office housed a half-dozen mismatched desks scattered haphazardly around the room. There didn't seem to be a reception desk, or anything to welcome a walk-in customer. In the back corner was a home gym setup and some free weights.

As she tiptoed across the ripped indoor-outdoor carpeting toward the only occupied desk, she'd taken in the gallery of Wanted posters with darts protruding from the faces and the stacks of magazines—*Soldier of Fortune*, *Guns & Ammo*, *Fast Car*—decorating the desks.

The only computer in the room was a big, beige clunker grimy with fingerprints.

But then she'd seen Rex. Although his face had not appeared in the magazine article she'd read, she'd somehow known instantly that the man seated behind a desk at the back of the room was Rex Bettencourt. With military-short, sun-bleached hair and a deep tan even in the dead of winter, his posture had communicated the sort of supreme confidence she was looking for. And from the moment he'd opened his mouth to speak, she'd known he was the man who could get her little girl back safe and sound. His impressive muscles made him look dangerous, but the intelligence behind his green eyes assured her he was also capable.

"You haven't given me much to work with," Rex said when he'd run out of questions. "A description of a woman who smokes with a rodent face and an accent isn't much help. Are you sure you've never seen this woman before?"

"I know I've never met her. But now that I've had a chance to think about it, to go over it in my mind, she seems familiar somehow. I may have seen her before—at a party, in a crowd."

"She might have been following you."

Nadia shivered at the idea of being watched. Her Russian grandmother had risked her life to come to this country, where she could be free, where her movements were not constantly monitored or her motives challenged. Nadia had been raised to appreciate her freedom, her relative safety.

Peter had taken that away from her.

"I know I haven't given you much," Nadia said. "But someone will be at the mall to spot me. Maybe it will be the woman again. You could follow her."

"If you spot her. Or if he doesn't send someone else, someone you wouldn't recognize."

"When he contacts me again, then," Nadia said.

"Peter probably won't send another messenger with a piece of paper. He'll try something different this time, maybe a phone call from a throwaway cell phone."

"He's bound to drop some kind of clue," Nadia said. "And if he doesn't, you can follow whoever picks up the package after I make the drop."

"If you aren't planning to give Peter what he wants, what will you put in the package?"

"Something that will look real enough that it will fool him for at least a while. He'll have the contents verified, but it will take some time. We have to find her before he discovers the truth."

"We'll do the best we can."

She searched his eyes, hoping to find reassurance there. But his expression was grim. "You're thinking he might have already hurt her."

"We have to consider all possibilities."

Nadia's eyes swam with tears. She did not want to hear this, yet she knew Rex spoke the truth. Peter was not honorable. He was a spy, a traitor to a country that had given him a chance, offered him sanctuary, embraced him as one of its own. He had no reason to keep Lily alive or deliver her unharmed, even if she gave him the Petro-Nano.

"I'm not trying to scare you," Rex said. "I'm just making sure you understand the terrible position we're in. He has all the cards. We have to find a way to upset the balance of power. And the first thing, I think, is to force him to open two-way communications."

"But I have no way of forcing him to do anything," Nadia said, calming down. Rex's commanding presence was almost comforting, despite the fact he was big and powerful and a little bit scary. Her experience with Peter had taught her just how much pain a man could inflict on a small woman like her. And Rex was taller, larger, undoubtedly stronger than Peter.

"We will find a way."

"Does that mean you're taking me on as a client?"

He looked slightly bemused. "I'm sure talking like that's the case."

Chapter Two

It wasn't the fanciest of plans, Nadia thought as she sat in the food court at Forest Ridge Mall, but Peter had left them few options. Nadia was frankly terrified of what would happen when Peter discovered she wasn't playing by his rules. But she'd put her fate in Rex Bettencourt's hands, and she'd agreed to let him make the decisions.

That didn't mean she was comfortable with the plan.

She had arrived at the time Peter had specified, wearing a red windbreaker over a red T-shirt. But she carried a small, hand-lettered sign that read, Must See Lily or No Deal. She had some leverage—she had something Peter wanted. The sooner she exerted her power, Rex had said, the better. And she should use that power to ensure her daughter was alive and well, which was their number-one priority.

Nadia tried not to look at Rex, who'd arrived at the food court a full hour ahead of her. He sat a few tables away, sipping a soft drink and talking to Gavin Schuyler, another bounty hunter. Rex had pulled a team together with amazing speed, and each of the other team members accepted their roles without question. Rex and Gavin would keep their eyes open for anything unusual. Peter, or one of his agents, had to be nearby to visually verify Nadia's presence.

Out in the parking lot, Beau Maddox was watching Nadia's Volvo. It had occurred to Rex that Peter, wanting to avoid phone calls or personal contact, might leave a communiqué on or near her car while she was safely inside the mall.

Back at the office, Lori, Rex's sister, was running through every possible avenue of computer research to locate Peter. She was also monitoring Nadia's cell phone. Nadia had privately wondered about Lori's qualifications, but Rex had assured her that in addition to being a black belt in Tae Kwon Do, Lori was a skilled hacker. If anyone could trace a call or turn up an e-trail for their suspect, Lori could.

Now they had to wait, and hope that Peter made a slip.

When Nadia's cell phone rang, she nearly upset her untouched soft drink. She fumbled with the phone, glancing to see whether Rex had noticed. He had. Though his gaze was never directly on her for more than half a second, she knew he was watching her.

"Hello?"

"You are in no position to make demands, sweetheart."

Inwardly shaking, Nadia gave a casual hand signal, indicating to Rex that she had Peter on the line. The call was being recorded via a device hidden inside her jacket.

"Oh, yes, I am," Nadia said. Everything inside her yearned to beg and grovel for Peter to return her child. But Rex had told her specifically not to do that. She had to pretend she was in perfect control. "I will give you what you want. But not without complete assurance that I will get Lily back safe and sound. Let me talk with her."

"You can talk with her after you—"

"No," she said sharply. "Once you deliver proof that Lily is safe, I will listen to your next demand. Not before." Then, though it was the hardest thing she'd ever done, she hung up. She knew she had to prove to Peter she was serious.

A few feet away, Rex was shocked that their power play had produced results so quickly. Peter Danilov must be desperate for whatever Nadia had. He might even be here at the mall himself.

The Forest Ridge Mall had three levels. The food court was on the bottom; the other two levels looked down upon it. Rex had guessed that Peter had chosen this location so he or a coconspirator could observe from a high perch. Rex scanned the people near the railings above him.

"There," said Gavin, pointing with his eyes. "Two o'clock to you. A blond guy in a black shirt, talking on a cell phone. His body language says he's angry."

Rex saw him. He could have been Peter Danilov, but Nadia had only been able to provide a grainy, outdated photo of her ex-husband. He had apparently taken all photos with him when they'd divorced, anticipating something like this. Lori was currently tracking down other photos—his employee ID picture, from when he'd worked at JanCo as a low-level lab tech, or his mug shot from when he'd been arrested for assaulting Nadia. But they hadn't arrived yet.

"Let's go," Rex said. Their plan was to follow a suspect, if they found one, which was one of the reasons Rex had brought Gavin with him. Two people could tail someone easier than one could, and with less chance of being spotted.

He didn't like leaving Nadia unprotected, but she'd been instructed to remain exactly where she was until she received a prearranged signal from him or someone on the team to return to her car.

As Rex and Gavin rode the escalator up to the second level where their suspect was, Rex spoke into his walkie-talkie headset, which resembled a cell phone accessory. "Beau, you copy?"

"I'm here."

"Any action around the car?"

"Nope."

Rex tamped down his irritation at Beau's less-than-military lingo on the walkie-talkie. Beau was an ex-cop, the emphasis being on *ex*. He didn't care for anything that smacked of rules and regulations, including radio codes. But no one could argue with Beau's results. He got the job done, and Rex couldn't think of anyone he'd rather have at his back.

"We've made a visual ID of a suspect. I'll need your help tailing him once he exits the mall. Blond guy in a black T-shirt, about six feet, one-eighty pounds—"

"Hold on," Gavin interrupted.

As they reached the second level, their suspect turned around and smiled as a redheaded girl about ten years old approached him. They hugged, and Rex could see the relief evident in his face. "I told you to wait for me at the bookstore," he scolded. "You scared me to death."

Gavin and Rex looked at each other. No wonder the man had been agitated on the phone—he'd lost his daughter. They could also both see, now that they'd gotten a good look at the man, that he was closer to fifty than forty—way too old to be Peter.

"Hell," Rex muttered. He spoke into the walkie-talkie again. "Cancel the previous. Wrong guy."

Rex headed for the down escalator, which descended through a forest of carefully sculpted trees still sporting their Christmas lights, though it was January. He peered through the trees, searching for Nadia's red jacket, feeling inexplicably anxious about having left her vulnerable, even for a couple of minutes.

Moments later, he realized his anxiety was perfectly well placed. Nadia was gone.

"Where'd she go?" Gavin asked, sounding as bewildered as Rex felt.

"Damn it!" He scanned the crowd for any sign of a red shirt and a curly mop of black hair.

"Maybe she went to the bathroom," Gavin said uncertainly.

"She wouldn't. I made myself pretty clear, didn't I? That she wasn't to move from that table? If she did, she must have had a good reason."

"You hardly know her," Gavin argued. "For her, maybe a call of nature *is* a good reason."

But Rex felt he did know her. Technically they'd met only four hours ago. But he'd seen that haunted look in the eyes of other women, other mothers who feared they would never see their children again. He might not know exactly how Nadia felt, but he understood how a woman in her situation thought. And she wouldn't take an unnecessary risk.

Had she been lured here for a kidnapping? But if that had been her ex-husband's goal, why stage it here in a crowd? Why not a more remote location?

"Hey, is that her?" Gavin asked, pointing to a speck of red far down the mall concourse.

Rex pulled a tiny pair of binoculars from his jacket and peered toward the retreating woman who walked side by side with a dark-haired man. He couldn't see her face, but he could tell by her walk that it was Nadia. As a sniper, he'd learned to identify people from a distance. Now it was second nature to catalog the way people walked, how they moved their hands when they talked, how they cocked their heads, how their hips swayed with— He pulled his mind back to the present.

"It's her," he confirmed. "Let's move."

They hurried down the concourse, breaking into a sprint as Nadia and her companion neared the entrance of a department store. The shoppers they breezed past gave them strange stares.

"Beau, you read?" Rex said into the walkie-talkie.

"Ten-four, good buddy."

"Change of plans. Nadia is heading into JCPenney with an unknown person. Male, six feet, one-seventy, dark hair."

"Dark hair?"

"Be ready to take over pursuit if they exit the store. Under no circumstances are you to allow Nadia to enter this guy's vehicle."

"Is SHE EATING?" Nadia asked, hurrying to keep up with Peter as he strode toward JCPenney. Her heart pounded and her skin was awash in goose bumps, and she had to resist the urge to look behind her to see if Rex was following.

She had disobeyed one of Rex's direct orders. She wasn't supposed to have moved from her table at the food court until he gave her the signal. But Rex and Gavin had both disappeared, and then there was Peter, his blond hair dyed brown, whispering in her ear the most seductive of songs: "You win. Come with me, and I'll let you see Lily."

She hadn't seen him coming. Peter always did have the ability to move quickly and silently, like a cat. When he'd told her that her baby was close by, her body had moved almost of its own accord, her mother's instincts craving contact with her offspring.

Her Nana Tania had always emphasized the need for flexibility when it came to matters of intrigue. Peter suddenly appearing in person was an unforeseen event, she reasoned. Rex would approve of her impromptu response, she was almost sure. This might be their best chance of recovering Lily. Rex would follow, and he would have help from Beau and Gavin.

Provided Rex had seen her leave with Peter. Oh, God, what if he hadn't? She wasn't in danger, though, really, was she? In this public place, what could he do? He hadn't pulled a gun, hadn't shown her any sign of force at all. He'd merely told her that his girlfriend was with Lily in another part of the mall, and this would be Nadia's one and only chance to see her daughter until after the Petro-Nano was delivered.

Peter set a zigzagging course through the department store, pausing often to see if anyone was following.

"I'm here alone," Nadia said, certain Rex wouldn't reveal his presence.

"You double-crossed me once," Peter said. "You'd do it again in a heartbeat if you thought you could get away with it." He paused long enough to look her in the eye in a way that made her shrivel inside. For a moment, all she could think about was the feel of his fist making contact with her face, the sickening thud-crunch, the explosion of pain and the keening scream that had sounded strange and alien, but which had come from her own throat. And she knew he would make her suffer for not meekly following his orders. If he knew she'd gotten help, if he knew she'd lied to him, his retribution would be that much worse.

Even if he had to exact it from a prison cell.

She shivered.

"All right. Come on. Lily is in my car with Denise."

Nadia hadn't counted on Peter taking her outside. She was afraid of what he might do in the relative isolation of the parking lot. But surely Rex and his buddies were watching.

As they exited the store into a cold, gray day, Nadia zipped up her inadequate windbreaker. The parking lot wasn't all that isolated, she realized with some relief. It was a busy Saturday afternoon. People were coming and going.

Then she noticed a blond woman heading toward her, and she tensed. Lori, Rex's sister. They'd left her back at the First Strike office doing computer searches. What was she doing here?

Lori was going to pass very close to them. But there was no reason to worry, Nadia thought. Peter wouldn't recognize her.

"Nadia?"

Lori had stopped squarely in front of them. Panicking, Nadia looked blankly at Lori. Was she going to just give away the game right here in front of Peter? Or, she thought giddily, had the team already recovered Lily?

"Nadia Penn, it is you, right? It's Annette, from Michigan?"

"Annette!" Nadia said, hoping she had inherited at least a smidgen of acting ability from Nana Tania. "I haven't seen you in a million years! You look different. Have you lost weight?"

"Only about fifty pounds." Lori came in for a hug and whispered in Nadia's ear, "We're getting you out of this." After releasing Nadia from the hug she said, bright and cheerful as could be, "Is this your husband? I thought I heard you were getting married."

"That must have been a while ago," Nadia said. "Peter and I are divorced. But we, uh, have a daughter. That's why we're, uh…" She was blathering. She had to get control of this thing. Peter, who'd looked merely annoyed by the interruption a moment ago, was starting to frown and turn red.

"Come on, Nad, I do not have all day," he said. "You can gossip with your girlfriend another time. Denise and Lily are waiting for us in the car."

"Oh, that Russian accent is so cute," Lori simpered. "You sound just like Boris Badenov from the Bullwinkle cartoon."

What in the hell was Lori doing? Nadia wondered wildly. Stalling, maybe, so the team could get into place? She was also making Peter angry. What if he took it out on Lily, or the hapless Denise, whoever she was?

"We really have to go," Nadia said with as much conviction as she could muster. How far were they from Peter's car? she wondered. How close was Lily?

"I'll walk with you," Lori said, sounding ridiculously perky. "I'd love to see your daughter."

Peter turned on Lori, his temper erupting. "Why don't you mind your own business, you stupid cow? This is a private matter."

"Hey, nice manners." Lori's chin jutted out, challenging Peter. "God, Nadia, no wonder you divorced him."

Without warning, Peter took a swing at Lori and Nadia reflexively screamed. But Lori blocked the blow with amazing agility, Peter's fist glancing harmlessly off her forearm. Realizing he'd tangled with more than he bargained for, Peter took off running.

Lori started to follow, but Nadia grabbed onto her arm. "No," she said insistently. "If you chase him, he'll know you're not just an old friend." Nadia watched in despair as her chance to see Lily vanished with Peter as he dodged in and out of the rows of cars.

Lori nodded, seeing the wisdom of Nadia's logic. "Beau's out here, too. He's in his car. He'll be able to follow Peter." Even as the words left her mouth, a black Mustang sped past them.

"Peter will know he's being tailed," Nadia said.

"Not if we double-team him. Come on, my car's over here."

Certain Peter was focused on escape and no longer paying attention to them, Nadia sprinted beside Lori's long-legged lope. "Why did you do that?" she demanded. "Why did you confront me? He was taking me to see Lily."

"It was too dangerous, letting Peter take you to his car. Strict orders from Rex not to let you go with him."

The burning in Nadia's lungs was the only thing that prevented her from dissolving into tears. She wouldn't be able to breathe if she started crying, and she had to keep up with Lori. Lori was going to chase Peter, and Nadia couldn't slow her down.

When they reached Lori's vehicle, an ancient gray van with mirrored windows, Nadia had her doubts that this old bucket of bolts could catch anything, but she climbed into the passenger seat.

Her doubts about the van melted when Lori started her up. Sounded like she had a souped-up V-8 under the hood. *"Batjushki,"* she murmured, borrowing one of Nana Tania's favorite curses. She quickly fastened her seat belt as Lori whipped out of her parking space with a roar and a screech of tires, driving the behemoth as if it were a sports car.

Lori grabbed the CB radio, driving with one hand. "Beau, this is Lori, you read?"

"Ten-four, Blondie. You got Blue Dog here, runnin' and—"

"Shut up with that stuff. What's your twenty? Over."

Beau sounded more serious when he answered. "Heading south on the service road. The target just crossed Augustine Road. Over."

"What's he driving? Over."

"Green Plymouth Reliant, older model. No license plates. You can't miss it. Over."

Nadia grabbed the mike out of Lori's hand. "Beau?"

"Push the button, hon," Lori said.

Right. "Beau?" she repeated. "This is Nadia. Can you see who's in the car with him? Um, over."

There was a pause before he answered. "There's no one else in the car, just Peter. I got a good look when he almost bashed into me. We've hit some traffic now. He's about five car lengths ahead of me."

The mike dropped out of Nadia's hand. There was no one in the car. Lily wasn't with Peter at all. He'd lied. The implications made her sick to her stomach. Peter had had something else in mind when he'd lured Nadia out here, something other than allowing her to see her daughter. If Lori hadn't intervened, she would be in Peter's car right now, under his complete control.

"I think I'm going to throw up," Nadia said.

"Roll down the window, then, 'cause I'm not stopping." To prove her point, Lori ran the next light, which was Augustine Road. "Look, I think that's Beau's Mustang up ahead. But this damn traffic! Maybe I can turn left under the freeway and find an alternate route." She veered to the left lane, but it was no use. The traffic had come to a standstill.

Beau cursed over the radio. "He's going over the median and into the U-turn lane. I'm boxed in, I can't follow."

"Neither can I," Lori moaned. "Rex, are you there? Gavin?"

There was a loud burst of static. Then, "Where the hell are you? What happened? Where's Nadia?" The angry voice was undeniably Rex's, and Nadia wanted to dissolve into the van's tattered upholstery.

"I've got Nadia," Lori said. "She's safe. Beau has the suspect's car in his sight. Over."

"Correction," Beau interjected. "I had the car in my sight. It's gone now."

Rex let loose with a string of curses over the radio. Nadia was sure the FCC would yank his license if they caught him. "We'll debrief back at the office," he concluded. "Now."

Nadia's whole body burned with shame a few minutes later as she pulled her Volvo into a parking spot next to Lori's in front of the First Strike offices. When she entered, she saw that Beau, Gavin and Rex were already there, along with a man she didn't recognize. He was a robust-looking guy in his fifties with a tan and very short, silver hair. All the men were discussing something in hushed voices. They went silent when Nadia joined them, and she imagined they all stared at her with accusing eyes.

Rex opened his mouth, but Nadia beat him to it. "I know, I screwed up."

"Monumentally." His face was hard as quartz crystal, his jaw working. She could tell he was forcing himself not to explode. "When I give an order, I expect it to be followed."

Lori put her hand on Nadia's arm. "Oh, Rex, shut up. This isn't the Marines. Peter said he was going to let her see her baby out in the parking lot."

"I th-thought you would see what was happening," Nadia added, feeling her excuse was a poor one. He was right to be angry with her—she shouldn't have gone against the plan they'd laid out.

The older man pulled out a chair for her. "I'm Ace McCullough. You want some coffee? You look a little shaken up."

"Some water. I can get it." She started to rise, but Lori pushed her back down in the chair.

"Just sit for a few minutes. I'll get your water." She shot an accusing look at her brother as she passed where he sat, perched on the edge of a desk.

Rex took a deep breath, his muscular chest expanding beneath his black T-shirt. Nadia slid out of her windbreaker in deference to the office's overactive heater.

"Okay," Rex said in a calmer voice. "Does Peter know Nadia went to someone for help?"

"I doubt he knew I was following," Beau said. "I never got close enough."

For the first time, Nadia noticed a huge black dog lying near Beau's feet. A Rottweiler, she thought, remembering a story her grandmother had once told her about being chased by a Rottweiler when she was part of the Russian occupation force in Germany. Nadia kept one eye on the enormous dog, and it seemed to be studying her with equal parts curiosity and suspicion.

"I doubt Peter was worried about me," Lori said as she returned with a glass of water and handed it to Nadia, who murmured her thanks. "I was playing the ditzy college friend. I think I just spooked him because I didn't cower and whimper when he tried to hit me."

"He hit you?" Rex sounded alarmed.

Lori shrugged it off. "I said he tried. He may be strong, but he's a totally unskilled fighter."

"He's a bully and a coward," Nadia interjected. "He wouldn't have stood up to you if he'd realized you could beat him up." The thought of a slender, pretty blonde beating the crud out of Peter pleased Nadia. "I wasn't able to fight back like you can, and that's what he's used to."

"I could teach you—"

"Focus, people," Rex said. "Lori, were you able to find anything useful on the computer?"

"Absolutely nothing. That's why I came out to the mall—I thought I could be more use to you there. Peter is hiding behind a pretty thick curtain. I've seldom seen anyone disappear as thoroughly as he has, unless they're dead. He must have support."

"Russian Mafia," Nadia murmured.

A collective groan rose up among the bounty hunters. "You didn't think it was important to mention this before?" Rex asked.

"I don't know for sure he's involved, but he must be working for someone," Nadia said. "Given his political leanings, it would make sense he's getting funds and support from someone or some group connected to Russia."

"This is a little…big," Ace said, "even for you, Rex."

Nadia could see Rex didn't like having his manly prowess questioned. But she also sensed he wouldn't let his ego get in the way of common sense.

"Maybe it's time to go to the authorities," Rex said grudgingly.

"Not the local cops," Gavin said, sounding alarmed. "Can you imagine the muddle Lyle Palmer could make of this case?"

"Who's Lyle Palmer?" Nadia asked.

Lori answered. "Only the most incompetent detective in the state. He hates us because we've shown him up a few times, and his sole goal in life is to find reasons to arrest us."

"I was thinking we should take it higher," Rex said. "Given the security level of Nadia's work and Peter's history, and the fact he's obviously not working alone, the FBI or even Homeland Security might be interested."

Nadia felt panic rising in her throat at the thought of bringing anyone else into the loop. "Peter will go ballistic if he finds out," she said. "You saw how he reacted today. When he thinks anything is going out of control, he reacts impulsively, and nothing would make him freak out faster than federal authorities. I'm afraid of what he might do to Lily if he gets frightened."

"I agree," Gavin said. "He sounds like a complete loose cannon. If we go through proper channels, God knows what kind of federal yahoo might get assigned to Nadia's case, blundering in like a trumpeting elephant."

Rex pursed his lips. The others looked thoughtful.

"I could call a couple of friends," Rex said. "Keep it unofficial. They could make quiet inquiries, see where there's been any mention in Russian communiqués of the possible acquisition of top-secret technology."

He looked at Nadia. "I'll let you make the decision."

"What's the alternative?" Nadia asked.

"We keep hammering away on our own," he said.

"We have lots of areas we haven't explored, lots of ways to track Peter down. He must have friends, relatives, hobbies. He can be traced, and if we're smart about it and a little bit lucky, we'll find him and Lily."

Nadia felt the first stirrings of renewed hope. "He does have interests. I was married to him for three years. I know more about him than almost anyone."

Rex arched one eyebrow. "Then you're saying you don't want to bring in the authorities?"

She took a deep breath. "Not yet. I made a demand— asking to see Lily. I want to give him a chance to comply with that demand. By changing the rules, we've got him off balance. If he doesn't produce proof that Lily is alive, we can assume—" she swallowed, her throat suddenly dry as she was reminded of just what was at stake "—we can assume he isn't able to. Then it won't matter who we call. CIA, FBI, National Guard. Anybody we can think of. Anyone who'll shoot to kill."

Chapter Three

While Rex and Ace went through their lists of U.S. intelligence contacts, and with Nadia's approval made some very cautious and diplomatic inquiries, Nadia sat down with pen and paper. Rex had given her instructions to make a list of everyone Peter knew. Then another list of his hobbies and interests. And a third of any place he frequented—churches, stores, bars. Rex had told her to write down everything that came to mind, no matter how trivial.

Twenty minutes later, Rex was off the phone and Nadia had three formidable lists. She was surprised at how many potential leads she had come up with. Rex gathered the bounty hunters together again and they went over Nadia's lists.

"Peter thinks very highly of himself," Nadia said when she was given the floor. Rex had asked her to describe his personality and habits to the rest of the team. "He is very superior. He has good taste, or thinks he does, and he considers most Americans to be pigs. He likes fine French wine. And vodka, of course. He only smokes Cuban cigars, which he gets from Russian friends."

"So, are most of his friends Russian?" Beau asked.

"Yes. He belongs to a society, sort of like a secret club or lodge, that admits only those born in Russia. I don't even know what it's called, but you could probably find it through the Russian Orthodox church on Jersey Street."

"Did he go to that church?" Gavin asked.

"No, he wasn't remotely religious. But the church has close ties to the lodge."

She went on to name the two friends Peter hung out with at work—young intellectuals with a radical bent. "They talked about Russian literature and politics. They're young men, early twenties, I think, and they idolized Peter. He liked to hang out with people he could control."

"Is that why he married you?" Rex asked.

It was an honest question, but it made Nadia uncomfortable to admit that, yes, for a while he was able to control her. "He dazzled me, especially at first. I admired his intelligence and his fierce ideals, even though they were different from mine. But he chose me because I had access to technology he wanted. It was that simple. Once I realized that, he had no power over me. But by then it was too late. I had told him more than I should have about my work, and that made me vulnerable."

She hesitated, then added, "This isn't the first time he's tried to get secrets out of me. I should have turned him in when I found out what he wanted. But then there were the threats and the violence…he promised to stay out of my life if I kept my mouth shut."

Nadia had just revealed far more than she'd meant to.

She was supposed to be relating Peter's friends and interests, not justifying her stupidity.

But she saw no condemnation in the bounty hunters' faces as they listened to her story with rapt attention. She thought she even saw understanding in Rex's eyes.

She felt lighter, having admitted her past mistakes. She hadn't realized how deep-seated her guilt was until now.

"If I had turned Peter in," she finished, "I would not be here now."

"You couldn't have known that," Lori said. "You made the best decision you could at the time. We just have to move forward now, not look back."

"Let's focus, people," Rex said again. "This isn't *Oprah*. Nadia, what else is on your list?"

"He loves guns," Nadia continued, moving quickly past Rex's rebuke. He was right, of course. They did need to stay focused on the here and now. "He is a very good marksman, and he even took some trophies at a few tournaments."

"Did he belong to the Payton Gun Club?" Ace asked.

"Yes. It's on my list. I even went there a few times myself, for target practice."

"So you can handle a gun," Lori said with renewed respect.

"Yes, I know firearms," Nadia said modestly. "My grandmother was a…a collector. She taught me to shoot. I got rid of all my guns when Lily was born, though. I couldn't stand the thought that someday she might… well, I'm sure you've heard the statistics."

"We know," Gavin said. "Beau and I both have young children."

That surprised her. The idea that these tough guys had wives, families, seemed incongruous. Her gaze flickered toward Rex, trying to picture him as a dad, playing softball with his kids, enjoying a backyard barbecue. The picture wouldn't come.

"Peter had friends at this club?"

"Yes. Another Russian, Vlad. I don't remember his last name. After I lost interest in shooting, Peter hung out at the club even more. He started participating in the hunts, where they would release an animal onto the grounds and the hunters would compete to see who could track it and kill it first."

Lori made a face. "That's really sick."

"I thought so, too," Nadia agreed. "But they were very popular events. Peter said there was no greater high than the thrill of the chase." Though these details about Peter seemed off the subject to Nadia, the bounty hunters were all taking notes or at least listening carefully.

"Do you have any other names from the club?" Rex pressed.

"There was a woman...." She paused. Could that be it? Could that be where she'd seen the rat-faced woman? She'd gone to a wine-and-cheese function shortly before she'd dropped out.

"Nadia, what is it?" Rex asked.

"That might be where I saw the rat-faced woman. I vaguely remember a woman, a Russian accent. She was flirting with Peter, but I was so used to that happening that I just tuned it out. But she had dark hair, not blond."

"People can change their hair color," Rex pointed out. "At any rate, this Payton Gun Club sounds like it's worth checking out."

"I have a membership," Ace said, which didn't surprise anyone. "I know the owner. Rex, I'll get you a guest pass."

REX DIDN'T WASTE ANY TIME. He culled the most promising leads from Nadia's list, and parceled out the assignments. He sent Lori to check out the former co-workers, since they were young and male and kind of nerdy, in Nadia's opinion. They would respond to a pretty blonde.

Ace volunteered to go to the Orthodox church and see what he could find out about the Russian lodge. "I speak a little Russian," he said, though he was vague about how he had acquired the skill.

Beau was assigned the fancy smoke shop where Peter got his illegal Cuban cigars. The guy who ran the store was one of Peter's friends. Gavin offered to check out Peter's last known address and canvass the neighbors.

"That leaves the gun club for you and me," Rex said to Nadia. "We'll go first thing in the morning."

"I'm going with you?"

"I can't leave you alone, unprotected," Rex said. "Peter already tried to kidnap you once. He might have decided blackmailing you using Lily is too risky, since you're not playing by the rules. Rescuing one hostage is difficult enough. I don't aim to have to rescue two."

Though Rex's protectiveness was strictly practical in nature, it warmed her nonetheless. It had been a very long time since anyone had shown concern for her welfare. And though she knew she was buying all this concern, she liked it. It made her feel secure in a way she hadn't experienced since Nana Tania's death.

"Tonight," he continued, "you'll stay in a hotel. I can be sure no one follows you there."

"That's not really necessary," she argued. "My house is very sec—" She stopped when she saw the uncompromising look in Rex's eyes. "Right. A hotel."

"HOW DID YOU SLEEP?" Rex asked as Nadia climbed into his black Blazer the next morning. She'd managed to acquire some fresh clothes, he noticed. Same jeans, but now she wore a Southeast Texas State University sweatshirt under her windbreaker, probably acquired from the hotel gift shop.

She plugged her cell phone into his cigarette lighter to recharge. "I managed a couple of hours."

"I take it you didn't hear from Peter?"

"Not a peep." She looked at him anxiously. "What if we did the wrong thing? What if he's broken off communications for good?"

"How bad does he want this…thing you have?"

"Bad."

"He'll call. He's just licking his wounds."

"But what about Lily? Twenty-four hours have passed now."

Rex knew the statistics as well as anyone. But he didn't think they applied here. Peter Danilov was a blackmailer, not a sex fiend. He had a stake in keeping Lily alive. "He'll call."

He needed to distract Nadia from her morose thoughts. "I need you to tell me what you know about the Payton Gun Club." He'd done quite a bit of research last night, but she might have some insights.

"Well, it's been around for more than a hundred years," Nadia said. "It used to be a huge estate belonging to one of the town founders—I forget what his name was. But he was really into hunting, and I guess he didn't have children because he left his entire estate to the city of Payton, with the condition that the land and home be preserved and left undeveloped for use by hunters."

"How big is it?" Rex asked.

"Several hundred acres. The Payton Gun Club leases the land from the city. The club renovated the barn, then built onto it for its shooting range and administrative offices. But no one had any money to keep up the old house, so now it's just a crumbling ruin they use for tactical exercises. The rest of the grounds have been left wild. There's a tall fence around the perimeter, and barriers to prevent stray bullets from getting off club property. But mostly it's just wilderness."

"And when they have these live hunts—how does that work?"

"They bring in some deer or javelina hogs or whatever, tag them and turn them loose. Then they turn the hunters loose."

Rex had to agree with Lori—it did seem barbaric. The animals hardly had a chance, trapped in an enclosed area, even if it was hundreds of acres.

The Payton Gun Club was in a rural area outside the

city limits. Though Nadia had described it, Rex wasn't prepared for the actual place, starting with the wrought-iron fence that ran along the road for a half mile before they actually reached a gate and a discreet sign identifying the place. The peeling sign said Members Only in large letters, but the rusty iron gates were open, so Rex drove in. The Blazer's tires crunched over the limestone gravel drive.

A smattering of cars was parked in the lot in front of a barnlike structure. Behind the barn was a long cinder-block building with no windows—had to be the indoor shooting range. Through a chain-link fence, Rex could just make out some targets in the distance—an outdoor range, probably not used much in the winter. Farther in the distance, a gray stone house rose up out of the prairie grass and scrubby trees. With its vacant windows and sagging roof, it had to be the former owner's home, fallen into disrepair.

Beyond the house were woodlands. At least the poor animals had some place to hide.

"This place gives me the creeps," Rex said. He made no move to exit the car as he tried to get a feel for the club. Maybe he'd seen too many spooky movies as a kid, but the Payton Gun Club had an air of shabbiness and desolation that called to mind maniacal killers in hockey masks. Especially that house. "You used to come here, huh?"

"I like target shooting," she said. "It sounded like fun. But really, I only came a couple of times. I was never comfortable here, and Peter was just as happy to have me stay home so he could have male bonding moments with his friends. Female bonding, too, if I'm right about rat-face."

"So you don't think you'll be recognized?"

"Doubtful."

Just the same, he had Nadia pull her distinctive curly hair back with an elastic, then wear a baseball cap and her sunglasses. It was enough to throw off a casual observer, anyway.

Just inside the barn's double doors was a reception desk. A bored-looking kid sat behind it reading a comic book. "Hi," Rex greeted him, causing the kid to jump. "Ace McCullough left a couple of guest passes for me and my wife?"

"Oh, yeah, they're around here someplace.…" The kid rummaged around on the desk until he found them. "Dennis and Freesia Blankenship?"

"That's us."

"I'll need some ID," the kid said, sounding bored.

"Oh, Dennis, I left my purse in the car," Nadia said.

"That's okay," Rex said. "I've got my license." And he did, in fact, have a fake driver's license. It was Rex's picture, but Dennis's name. The kid gave the card a cursory look and jotted down the number which, if anyone checked, would come back as belonging to a deceased person. But he doubted anyone would check. No one ever did.

Rex told the kid they were there to do some target practice with a gun he was thinking of buying. The kid handed them some ear-protectors, assigned them a lane and pointed them in the direction of the indoor range.

The range was bigger than it looked from the outside.

And despite the rather shabby exterior, the inside appeared to be state of the art. They found their lane. And while Rex opened the leather case he'd brought and looked at the huge .44 Magnum Ace had loaned him, Nadia covertly checked out the other three shooters.

"I don't recognize any of them," Nadia said.

But Rex did. One of them was a Payton police officer, a young patrolman not long out of the Academy who hung around Lyle Palmer and tried to earn brownie points. Andy Arquette, that was his name. Rex did his best to keep his back angled toward Andy, not wanting a confrontation.

Rex wondered why a cop would come here when the police had their own shooting range he could use for free.

Nadia gave a low whistle when she saw the gun. "A Ruger Super Blackhawk .44 Magnum. That is some fancy handgun. I love the blue steel."

"Your granny must have been quite a knowledgeable collector."

"Well, actually, Nana Tania was a spy." Some people reacted strangely to that information, but Rex took it in stride, nodding appreciatively. "After she retired, she said she was glad to be out of the spy business, but she must have missed it some, because she had a closet full of guns. When I was little, we would take them out and play with them the way other little girls take out their Barbie collections."

Rex just shook his head. "You'll have to tell me more about your Nana sometime. So, can you shoot this baby?"

She demurred. "I'm really rusty—haven't touched a firearm since Lily was born. You go ahead."

He'd been afraid of that. But if they wanted this to look good, they would have to actually fire the gun. He took the wicked-looking blue-steel gun out of its foam nest and loaded one of the many full magazines Ace had included. It clicked into place with a satisfying snick.

A paper target was about fifteen yards down the lane. Rex and Nadia put on their ear protection. Nadia stood back, giving Rex plenty of room. He took a wide-legged stance, put both hands on the gun, stretched out his arms and took aim. But his hands were shaking, and perspiration had broken out on his upper lip and forehead despite the range's cool temperature. For a few moments, he thought he wouldn't be able to shoot at all. He thought his stomach would rebel. But somehow, he managed to squeeze off the first shot, then another and another.

That was when the panic started welling up inside his chest. It was the sound of the gunfire, he realized. In the four years he'd been a bounty hunter, he had never discharged his weapon. He'd drawn it and intimidated people with it, as he had Jethro Banner just a couple of days ago. But he hadn't actually squeezed the trigger until just now.

He laid the gun down, pulled off the ear protection and stepped back.

"Let's see how you did." It was Andy Arquette, who'd approached while Rex was shooting. Andy pushed the button that would bring the paper target close for inspection. "Haven't seen you around here before. Name's Andy Arquette."

It appeared that Andy didn't recognize him, Rex

thought. Good. "Dennis Blankenship." The two men shook hands. "This is my wife, Freesia." Hell, Nadia didn't look like a Freesia. Ace had a damnable sense of humor.

She mustered a smile and a quick handshake.

The paper target arrived. Rex didn't even want to look at it, because he'd practically shot at the thing with his eyes closed. But when he did look, he saw that three of his five shots had actually hit—one in the arm, one in the abdomen, one in the thigh.

"Ooh, that guy's hurting," Andy said charitably. He was a tall, skinny guy with straight black hair. Rex didn't like the way he was looking at Nadia.

"I've never shot this gun before," Rex said, feeling he needed to rationalize his lousy marksmanship.

"Why don't you give it a try…Freesia," Andy said. Something about his tone bothered Rex. Was there a slight challenge to the suggestion?

"It's an awfully big gun for a lady," Rex said, trying to give Nadia an out. She'd said she didn't want to shoot.

But she surprised him. "I'll give it a try." With the push of a button she sent the target out to the same distance at which Rex had shot it. Then, after a short hesitation, she pushed the button again, sending it even farther.

"You sure?"

Wordlessly she put on her ear protection, and Rex followed suit. Rather than the wide-legged stance Rex had taken, she stepped one foot back and planted it in a wide lunge. Then she aimed, sighting down the barrel with one eye, her face a mask of total concentration.

She pulled the trigger, then kept on pulling it until the

magazine was empty. Though the gun had a colossal kick, Nadia hardly seemed to notice it. Her unconventional posture seemed to work well for her.

She laid the gun down, pulled off the ear protection, then pushed the button to bring the target close once again.

Rex's blood drained to his feet when he got a good look at the target. Every one of Nadia's shots had hit the paper man in the head.

"Damn." Andy barely breathed the word. "Freesia, you're not a member here, are you?"

"No, just a guest."

"We could sure use you on our coed team. Lemme show you around—maybe y'all will want to join."

"Sure, we'd love to look around," Nadia said. That was why they'd come, after all—to nose around, find out if anyone had seen Peter recently.

Rex packed up the Magnum.

"You can check that into a locker if you don't want to carry it around," Andy said. "The lockers are free."

"That's all right, I'll keep it," Rex replied.

Andy showed them around the building. They'd already seen most of it, except for a small lounge area, which was currently empty. "Members are encouraged to socialize here—but only after they're done shooting for the day. The owners are very strict about alcohol use."

They went through a set of double glass doors to the outdoor range. Two men in camouflage with an arsenal of hunting rifles stood around, discussing the merits of their guns, but otherwise it was quiet.

"There's a trap range on the other side of that earth barricade, and also a forty-yard tin-can range."

They walked a little farther until they reached a small metal shed near a gate. Andy led them toward it and opened the door. "We keep reflective vests stored in here for the members' convenience. We recommend you wear them. The wilderness area is over four hundred acres, and you never know who might be out here with a gun. You don't want to be mistaken for a wild pig."

They donned the neon orange vests and walked into the wilderness as Andy explained about the bountiful dove, quail, ducks and pheasants the members bagged. "Rabbit and squirrel are fair game year round," he added with a grin that set Rex's teeth on edge. "Good eatin'."

They tromped farther out. Rex kept looking for an opening, a way he could casually ask about Peter, but he didn't trust Andy, who seemed far too friendly, so he had to proceed with caution.

Andy pointed out the crumbling old mansion. "Game likes to hide in there," Andy said. "One time during a javelina hunt, I cornered something in there with red eyes, and I thought I had me a pig. It turned out to be a possum."

"They make a good stew," Rex said, trying to get into the spirit of the conversation, though hunting animals had never appealed to him. He found it much more sporting to hunt something with an equivalent level of intelligence to his.

"So, who referred you to the Payton Gun Club?" Andy asked conversationally.

"Ace McCullough," Rex answered. "He's been a member a long time."

"I've heard of him, of course," Andy said. "He's kind of a legend. Never met him, though."

"I know another guy who's a member here," Rex said. "Peter Danilov?"

"Oh, yeah, sure, I know Peter. He's out here a lot."

Was there just the tiniest hesitation when Andy answered? "You know, I tried to get hold of that guy recently, and the number I had for him was no good. I thought maybe he'd moved away. Has he been around lately?"

"Yeah, I saw him a coupla weeks ago," Andy said. "When I see him again, I'll tell him to get in touch with you."

"And that friend of his, Vlad—ah, hell, I can't remember his last name."

"I know who you're talking about. I couldn't tell you his last name, either—all those Russian names sound alike to me," he added in a good-ol'-boy twang that didn't fool Rex.

Andy made a show of checking his watch. "Oh, hell, I gotta go. Y'all just take your time, have a good look around. Freesia, we'd love to have you on our team. You too, Dennis," he added as an afterthought.

Yeah, right. Maybe Rex would join the club after all. With some practice he could at least learn to shoot a paper man with some degree of accuracy, even if he couldn't shoot a real one.

"So," Nadia said as they scuffed their way along a faint path that wove through an open field of tall prairie grasses, "Peter's been here recently. If we had Vlad's last name…"

"We might be able to weasel it out of the front desk guy," Rex said, just as something whizzed by his left ear.

His reaction was instinctual and instantaneous. He threw Nadia onto the ground and fell on top of her. The distant report of a high-caliber rifle reached his ears before he'd finished falling.

Chapter Four

"Crawl," Rex ordered, easing his weight from her so she could push up to hands and knees. He positioned himself next to her, between her and the old house, which was where the bullet had come from. Somehow he dragged the gun case along with him, grateful he'd obeyed his instincts and not let Andy talk him into stowing the gun in a locker.

"We need cover," he said. "We need to make those trees."

Nadia didn't question him. She crawled, and she did it quickly. Rex hoped the tall prairie grass would conceal their movements, but if their marksman was any good, he would see the grasses rippling in their wake.

If he'd been the sniper, he'd have fired into the grass. But no more shots came.

Then Rex realized why. The gunman had been shooting at Rex. He couldn't risk shooting at grass because he might hit Nadia—and Peter needed Nadia.

They were thirty yards from the nearest trees. But Nadia was agile and covered the distance quickly. They plunged into the woods several yards before stopping to catch their breath.

"Is there a very stupid hunter out there?" Nadia asked in a hoarse whisper. "Or was someone shooting at us on purpose?"

"With us in these orange vests?" Rex whispered back. "I doubt it was an accident. Anyway, bird hunters use shotguns, not rifles." As Rex spoke, he pulled the Magnum from its case and loaded it with a fresh magazine. "Maybe I should give this to you."

"Don't be ridiculous. Shooting at a target is a lot different than defending against a live shooter."

She didn't know the half of it. If she had any idea of his history, she'd yank the gun out of his hand so fast…

"Someone must have been watching for me to show up," Nadia said. "That kid at the front desk, do you think?"

"My guess is Andy Arquette."

"He did seem a little…insincere," Nadia agreed.

"Did Peter have any contacts in law enforcement?"

"He used to get a speeding ticket at least once a week, and he never had to pay them," she said.

That was all Rex needed to know. "I'm willing to bet Peter's power base is right here. We guessed right."

"For all the good it will do us if we don't get out alive."

"We'll get out. But we need to move—as quickly and quietly as possible. And we need to get rid of these damn vests." The neon orange, designed to prevent hunting accidents, could have the opposite effect in their case. They shed the vests.

They couldn't get out the way they came in. That path involved too much open prairie, and Rex wanted to avoid the old mansion, which afforded their shooter an excellent bird's-eye view.

Rex knew approximately where they were on the property, based on a map he'd seen near the front desk. He also knew the only way they were getting out of this place alive was over the fence—unless they killed the person hunting them, and Rex didn't want to think about that. He'd had more than his fill of killing.

They cut through the woods, which was thick with undergrowth. It offered good cover but made for slow going. Tree branches and mesquite scrub scratched them as they blazed a path.

At one point they stopped to listen, as they'd been doing every few minutes. Before, they'd heard nothing. Now, Rex discerned two sounds that concerned him. One was a barking dog. It was a good bet some of the hunters who hung out here had tracking dogs. The other sound was unmistakably running water. Rex had seen a stream or river on the map, but he couldn't remember now precisely where it had run. They would probably have to cross it to get to the perimeter fence.

"Dogs," Nadia whispered.

"Let's keep moving."

Rather than avoiding the water, Rex headed for it. If they waded or swam in the steam, the dogs might lose their scent. Of course, they might freeze to death. It was maybe fifty degrees out, not terribly cold, but the water in streams around these parts came from mountain springs way up in Colorado and would turn them blue in no time.

When they reached the stream, it turned out to be a

very shallow, fast-running creek. They scrambled down the limestone bank as the dogs' baying—definitely more than one dog—grew louder.

Rex grabbed Nadia's hand. "Let's run along the creek. Maybe the dogs won't be able to follow our scent. At least it might slow them."

"Do you have the slightest idea where we are?" Nadia asked. "Because I don't."

"I know exactly where we are." It was an exaggeration, but he needed Nadia to be optimistic and confident. He couldn't afford for her to fall apart in despair.

They splashed along the stream for maybe a quarter mile, until the water got deeper and they couldn't move quickly enough. They climbed out on the opposite bank, using protruding rocks and roots and small bushes to pull themselves up. Then they started running again, shoes squishing with water.

"I can still hear the dogs," Nadia said, panting slightly. He was amazed at her stamina and wondered what she did to stay in shape.

"We can't be far from the fence now." And they weren't. He saw it looming ahead, and his heart sank. He'd been hoping to discover a chain-link fence with some sort of baffling behind it to prevent stray bullets from escaping the gun club's grounds. What he saw was a sheer sheet-metal wall, ten feet high and extending as far as he could see in both directions. With razor wire at the top.

Nadia stopped and stared at the fence. "*Bozhe moj,* we'll never get over that."

"It seems excessive for a hunting club," Rex observed, wondering why the Payton Gun Club needed this degree of fortification. It called to mind some crazy cult, preparing to barricade itself inside a fortified compound with lots of weaponry and await the revolution. But there was no time to ponder the gun club's motives. The dogs were getting closer—Rex could see them now. The foray into the creek hadn't fooled them—they were probably tracking their prey on the wind anyway.

Rex looked up and down the fence line until he spotted something promising. "How good are you at climbing trees?"

NADIA WAS ACTUALLY VERY GOOD at climbing trees, or she had been when she was twelve. She'd been something of a tomboy as a child. Her American grandfather in Michigan had owned an orchard, and she'd spent many a fall day climbing high into the branches to snag apples the pickers had missed. When she saw what Rex had in mind, she didn't hesitate. She kicked off her athletic shoes and socks and climbed barefoot, gripping the old pecan tree's trunk with her feet like a monkey, using the barest of handholds. The skill came back to her without effort. She even remembered not to look down.

Rex was right behind her—and the dogs right behind Rex. No sooner had he cleared the ground than two enormous black-and-tan hound dogs leaped through the underbrush toward them. Moments later they were at the bottom of the tree trunk, baying loudly. Fortunately their human counterpart—the one with the gun—was far behind.

Nadia headed for one high branch in particular that reached out almost over the perimeter fence. She could walk out onto it a short distance, holding on to a branch above her for balance, but soon she lost her handhold and she had to sit on her branch and scoot. Unfortunately, the branch bent lower and lower with her weight. By the time she reached the wall, she was below the top. This wasn't going to work.

But Rex had the solution. He had grabbed on to the sturdier branch above and was working his way toward her, hand over hand, as if he were on playground monkey bars. "Grab on to my leg!"

It seemed reckless, but she didn't have any alternatives. She grasped his leg. His calf muscles were rock hard beneath the denim of his jeans. As he maneuvered farther out on the branch, she had to lift her legs to prevent getting snagged on the razor wire. Then, amazingly, she was clear of the wall.

"Jump!" Rex called.

During the split second she hesitated—the ground was a long way below—a shot rang out. That was all the urging she needed. She let go, plunging to the hard earth. Rex fell with amazing agility right next to her, dropping and rolling.

"You okay?"

She wasn't. She'd twisted her damn ankle. But she told him she was fine, and they got up and resumed running. They could hear the dogs running at the fence, barking furiously and banging into the metal in frustration.

"The road's this way," Rex said. "Give me your cell phone."

Her cell phone! All this time, she could have called 9-1-1 for help. But if that Andy Arquette was part of the conspiracy, what kind of story would he have told the cops when they arrived? Probably she and Rex would have been arrested for trespassing or something equally ludicrous. She handed the phone to Rex.

They slowed to a brisk walk as he phoned some-one at First Strike and relayed their approximate lo-cation. Five minutes later, they emerged from the woods onto a gravel road. Five minutes after that, they saw a car heading for them. Nadia's stomach tightened.

"Beau's Mustang," Rex said. Nadia realized they were going to live after all, and she almost dissolved with intense relief.

They climbed into the back seat of the black muscle car. Beau was driving, and Gavin was in the passenger seat, holding a gun. Beau pulled a U-turn, gravel pop-ping and flying, and he left a rooster tail of dust behind them. Nothing was said until they reached a main road.

"What in hell was that all about?" Beau finally asked.

Rex told the story, and Gavin gave a low whistle. "Sounds like those guys weren't kidding around."

"No, they weren't." Nadia rubbed her sore ankle. It wasn't too bad. Then she noticed that Rex was holding his right hand over his left arm. She pulled his hand away. It was covered with blood.

"Oh, Rex! You've been hit! You need a doctor."

"It's just a graze," he said, acting the typical macho male.

"You're bleeding all over everything!" She tried to examine the wound, but his leather jacket, with a neat bullet hole in it, was in the way. "Take the jacket off."

Just then, Nadia's phone rang, temporarily halting the argument. The car went very quiet. Nadia fumbled in her windbreaker for the phone and showed Rex the Caller ID display. It was a blocked call.

"Answer it," Rex said. He leaned close to her so he could hear both sides of the conversation.

Heat radiated from him, along with the clean, male smell from his exertion. She blocked those sensual signals from her mind as she pushed the talk button on her phone.

"What the hell is going on with you?" were Peter's first, outraged words. "What are you doing hanging out with a bounty hunter?"

"I'm sorry, Peter, I—" Rex pulled the phone away from her mouth, shook his head and made a fist, reminding her she needed to be strong, forceful, not a victim. "Rex is my boyfriend," she said boldly.

"I told you what would happen—"

"You said no cops. He's not a cop."

"Get rid of him! If I see him near you again, so help me—"

"After you tried to kidnap me at the mall, I thought I needed protection. And clearly I was right. Someone was shooting at me! He could have killed me, and then how would you get your precious nano?"

He didn't answer. Nadia felt sick to her stomach as she imagined a bullet ripping through her body.

"Why were you at the gun club?" Peter demanded.

"I was looking for you. Just tell me where you are, Peter. There is no need for all this cloak-and-dagger. I'll give you what you want. As I've told you repeatedly, the project is years and years away from producing actual, usable results. It won't do you any good."

"My sources tell me otherwise. If I tell you where I am, your *boyfriend* will shoot me down like a dog."

"Then prove to me Lily is safe. Let me talk to her."

"She's safe. I'm not a monster. But she's not here. Denise is taking care of her."

"Send me a video of Lily, then. Deliver it to my house." Rex was frantically tapping his watch. "By midnight tomorrow. If I see she's okay, I'll give you the nano."

"Get rid of the bounty hunter," Peter countered.

"Not going to happen. And if you don't get me that video, I'll go to the security director at JanCo, then together we'll go to the CIA. They'll listen to us, Peter. Do as I say."

She was watching Rex the whole time. He nodded his encouragement, then indicated she should hang up. She did, then sagged against the Mustang's leather interior, exhausted from the tension.

"Good, Nadia, that was good," Rex said in an almost crooning voice.

She hadn't realized she was holding her breath until she let it out in a gusty sigh. She'd done it. She'd actually stood up to Peter. And she'd unnerved him. She could tell by the uncertainty in his voice. It felt wonderful.

Rex's approval felt wonderful, too.

Gavin was already on his cell phone to Lori, who was back at the office trying to trace the call. "Peter was calling from a pay phone," Gavin said, relaying the report from Lori.

"He'll be long gone by the time we could get there," Beau said.

"What do we do next?" Nadia asked, suddenly energized by her own power. "Besides taking Rex to a doctor?"

REX'S INJURY LOOKED WORSE than it was. The exertion of running through the woods had caused it to bleed a lot, but the bullet had only grazed his arm. He'd had many such wounds in his life, and he was inclined to slap a bandage over it, change his shirt and move on.

But Nadia wouldn't hear of it. "Do you have any idea what kind of infection you could get?" she groused as he sat on his desk back at the First Strike office, shirtless, while Nadia cleaned the wound with peroxide.

Rex's arm jerked with the sting. "Ow. That hurts worse than the bullet did."

"Stop being a baby." But she blew on the jagged gouge, sending shivers of awareness coursing through his body to places not remotely injured.

He actually enjoyed her fussing over him. His mother had died when he was ten, and he couldn't recall any woman tending his cuts and scratches since then. Certainly not one this pretty. She darted in and out with her cotton balls and butterfly bandages, reminding him of a hummingbird. As she touched him with clinical indifference, his breathing became erratic and his head light. Maybe from loss of blood, but he didn't think he'd lost that much.

While Nadia tended him, Rex grilled the rest of the team about their progress. One of Peter's co-workers had quit JanCo and moved to California, Lori said, but she'd caught the other one at home the previous evening. He'd claimed not to have talked to Peter in months, despite Lori's determined flirtation and her tight, low-riding jeans. Gavin reported that Peter's old apartment had been cleaned out, and he'd left no forwarding address. None of the neighbors knew anything. Beau said the cigar store was no longer in business. Apparently the owner had gone back home to Russia. Beau did get his name—Vlad Popolov.

"Popolov," Nadia said suddenly, snapping her fingers. "That's the name—Peter's friend from the gun club. I hadn't realized they were the same person."

"Lori," Rex said, "see what you can dig up on this guy."

Ace had struck out at the church. "I found one guy sweeping up the place. He pretended not to speak English, and when I tried Russian, he pretended not to speak that, either."

"They're just naturally suspicious of outsiders," Nadia said as she finished up with gauze and tape. "There, I think you'll live, Rex. Does it still hurt?"

Yes, but he shook his head. Lori rolled her eyes. She'd been giving him looks over the top of her monitor ever since he and Nadia had walked in together. Lori had always been able to tell when he had a crush on a girl, even when she'd been a little kid.

"So what do we do next?" Nadia asked as Rex found a clean T-shirt in his desk drawer and put it on.

"You told Peter to deliver the video to your house," he said. "So we should wait there. Are you uncomfortable with my staying at your house?"

"I… No. I don't want to be alone."

Lori came up to Nadia, threw a casual arm around her shoulders and whispered something. Nadia offered a shy smile. Rex could only guess what sort of baloney his sister was dishing, but hopefully she was reassuring Nadia she had nothing to fear from him, despite his size and his rough bearing—and the fact that he'd developed an itch for his client, something only he and Lori knew.

Rex always kept a duffel bag at the office filled with essential toiletries, a couple of days' worth of clothes and some extra firepower, so it was never any trouble to take off on short notice.

He grabbed the duffel now and looked expectantly at Nadia. "I'll follow you. I'll be driving a black Subaru Outback until I can get the Blazer back from the gun club parking lot." It was Ace's spare he kept at the office, since the bounty hunters tended to lose or damage their cars on a regular basis. "Try not to lose me."

Lori snorted. "As if."

Beau's Rottweiler, Sophie, pushed to her feet, ears perked. She watched Rex expectantly, which gave him an idea. "Beau, can I borrow Sophie?"

"Sure."

"Sophie?" Nadia asked, instantly alert again. "Oh, the dog. You're going to bring that horse to my house?"

Beau pointed at Nadia. "Sophie? Friend."

Sophie lumbered closer, wagging the stump of her tail.

Nadia inched closer to the dog, which watched her carefully. "You're sure she won't bite me?"

"Now that she knows you're one of the good guys, she'll be harmless as a puppy to you."

"A big puppy," Nadia said.

Rex gave the dog a hearty slap on the rump, which didn't faze her. "But she would bite Peter if he showed up at your house unannounced. She's the extra pair of eyes and ears we need."

Nadia got close enough to pet the dog. Sophie seemed to enjoy the attention. She leaned against Nadia's leg and nearly knocked her over. "Whoa. Nice doggy."

"Let's move," Rex said.

Nadia nodded. He was grateful she didn't ask any questions or second-guess the plan. He realized he'd been a little hard on her yesterday, when he'd lit into her for leaving the mall food court. He hoped she understood now how important it was not to deviate from a plan once he'd established one.

He could understand, though, how her intense need to see her daughter had overridden her common sense. He didn't have any kids—at least, he hoped not—so he couldn't truly empathize with parental instincts. But he knew about wanting to protect someone. He'd been watching out for Lori since she was born. If something happened to her—if she were threatened in any way— he might not be so rational.

He watched as Nadia climbed into her efficient little station wagon with calm, capable movements. All things considered, she was holding it together pretty well. He checked the street for any cars that didn't belong, any people who looked out of place. In this neighborhood, with its scraggly inhabitants, anyone who was too well-groomed or who drove a clean car was suspect. But he saw only the usual—Ozzie the wino; Millie the panhandler, who carried a sign saying she needed money to feed her children when she didn't have any children; a couple of punks with a truck full of stuff to sell at the pawnshop, probably stolen.

Nothing unusual.

Chapter Five

Rex followed Nadia's car at a safe distance, surprised when she turned into Skylark Meadows, the same upscale community Beau lived in. Beau had scored a million-dollar reward for bringing a teenage heiress home safe, and he'd invested most of it in a luxurious minifortress. Nadia was apparently one of his neighbors.

The Volvo pulled into the driveway of an ultracontemporary, white-stucco home built on a hilly lot and surrounded by trees—the way most of the Skylark homes were. She obviously made a pretty decent living as a scientist, Rex thought. He wondered if she had a Ph.D. Probably. Dr. Nadia Penn.

Though he saw no cars on the street at all, he drove past Nadia's house just to be sure he wasn't being tailed. Then he turned around and pulled into her driveway and around the back. She was waiting in her car near the closed garage door, exactly as he'd instructed. Maybe he was being paranoid, but better paranoid than dead. He hadn't wanted to take on the responsibility of protecting a woman from danger. But now that he had, he was going to do it right.

He got out of his SUV, and Nadia rolled her window down, awaiting instructions. "You can open it now," he said. She punched a remote control on her visor and the double-garage door rolled open. "Sophie, check it out."

The Rottweiler jumped out of Rex's SUV and streaked into the garage, running from corner to corner and sniffing wildly. But there wasn't much to sniff. Inside, the garage was fastidiously clean and almost empty, save for a couple of ladders, an extension cord and a plastic garbage can. No chance anyone could hide in here. Perhaps that was why she kept the space so neat. He motioned her inside, then drove his own car in.

He and Sophie went into the house ahead of Nadia and checked out every space large enough for a person to hide in, noting as he made his way through the roomy house that Nadia had to be the neatest person he'd ever met. Most of the time, if you entered someone's house when they weren't prepared for visitors, you were likely to find piles of laundry, dirty dishes, or toys scattered about. Nadia's home looked as if it was ready for a magazine spread. Only Lily's bedroom showed any signs of clutter, and then it was only a few toys on the rug and a wrinkled bedspread.

When he was sure all was safe, he returned to the garage and escorted Nadia inside. "Sorry for all the cloak-and-dagger," he said. "But I believe in erring on the side of caution."

She nodded her understanding. "You're not being too cautious. That's not possible where Peter is concerned. I'm glad you aren't underestimating him." As she walked inside, she hung her purse and jacket on hooks inside a vestibule, then continued into the kitchen, switching on lights as she went. "Would you like something to drink? Maybe a sandwich?"

"You don't have to wait on me," Rex said. "I'll take care of myself. Unless you'd rather I stay out of your kitchen." Some women were funny that way.

"No, please, whatever you need..." She gestured vaguely, then looked down, obviously embarrassed. "This is awkward."

"It doesn't have to be," Rex said, trying to put her at ease. "You can just ignore me unless the phone rings or someone comes to the door."

"You're a little hard to ignore." Their eyes met and held for an instant longer than was comfortable. Rex wondered if he imagined the spark of awareness, the significant pause that lingered in the air like the tantalizing whiff of a rare scent. Probably all in his mind, he decided.

"You know, a sandwich sounds good." He started opening cabinets until he found some canned soup. Maybe they would both relax a little if they had something to keep them busy. "I'll make us some clam chowder."

Nadia seemed pleased by his suggestion. Utterly comfortable in her large, functional kitchen, she gathered cold cuts from the stainless-steel refrigerator and piled them on the granite-topped island. From a maple bread box she pulled a loaf of some whole-grain bread and cut thick, soft slices from it. Rex, meanwhile, rummaged until he found a saucepan and dumped the canned soup into it. They worked in companionable silence.

"I'm not used to having guests," she said after a

while. "After the divorce, I sold or gave away almost everything that held any memories of Peter. I painted the walls, took out the old carpeting, started clean—new furniture, new dishes, everything. This home has been my haven, the one place I felt safe from him. I've never invited anyone over. Not ever."

"I must seem like an invader, then."

"Actually, you make me feel safe."

Her answer pleased him. He wanted to help her, not cause her yet more stress.

They ate thick ham-and-Swiss-cheese sandwiches at a breakfast nook that overlooked a walled patio where a waterfall fountain sparkled in the winter sun. A lonely sparrow was filling up at one of the finch feeders.

Nadia made a valiant effort to eat, but she managed only about half of what was on her plate. Her stomach was probably tied in knots. Rex, on the other hand, was ravenous. Like an athlete preparing for a peak performance, he always ate a lot when in the middle of any operation. The thinking, the planning, the constant alertness burned as much fuel as if he were running a marathon.

Rex searched for some neutral topic of conversation. "You have a lot of bird feeders in your yard."

"I feed the birds all winter. Lily loves them. She sits at this table and shrieks with pure delight when they come to the feeders. That scares them away, of course, but they come back." She paused, shredding a crust of bread. "You didn't want to take my case. Why?"

He shrugged, as if her observation were of little consequence. "I was about to take a vacation," he said, because it was partly the truth. "Tahiti."

"I'm sorry I messed that up for you."

"I could have said no." Maybe he should have.

"I wouldn't have let you do that without a fight. I knew you were the right man for this job."

"I haven't produced stellar results so far."

"But you will."

Rex debated dashing her hopes. But in the end, he decided Nadia had a right to know the truth. It was her daughter's life at stake, after all, and maybe hers, as well. "Nadia, there's something you should know about me."

She looked at him with avid curiosity. "I think I know what I need to know. Unless the magazine article was wrong?"

"No, they got the *facts* right. But they didn't include the whole story, only the parts I wanted the reporter to know. I was intentionally vague about my past."

"You were Special Forces," she said. "I imagine much of what you did was classified. Or unpleasant. Or both. I don't blame you for not elaborating."

Unpleasant didn't begin to cover it. "I was a marine sniper." He watched her face, gauging her reaction, but she gave away little. At least she didn't look disgusted. "I killed people," he added, just to be sure she understood.

"They probably needed killing."

Her reaction so surprised him, he laughed, then quickly sobered. "Yeah, they did." He'd never killed anyone without a pretty damn good reason. Terrorism, child murder, genocide—the men he'd killed had résumés that could freeze camel spit. He'd believed, at least at the time, that his work could be justified because he was serving the higher good.

After his last assignment, though, he was never sure. The intelligence report had left out one crucial fact, which made him wonder what information had been left out of previous reports—or added in—to provide him with the proper motivation to kill.

"It doesn't bother me, the fact you've killed," Nadia said. "It may come down to that. If Peter forces my hand, I want someone at my back who knows how to pull a trigger."

And with that statement, she'd arrived neatly at the crux of the problem. He did not know if he could pull the trigger. But he would come back to that in a minute. "You seem rather matter-of-fact about a subject that makes most women—most men, too—squeamish."

Now she was the one to laugh, quick and harsh. "I'm not squeamish about much of anything."

"Because of Peter?"

"Partly. Once you've experienced getting your jaw broken, you don't fear pain as much because you know you can survive it. But you can give my grandmother credit for how I look at things. She raised me while my mother worked. And while other kids' grandmothers read them *Winnie the Pooh* and *The Cat in the Hat,* mine told me spy stories. Real spy stories. Not the sanitized James Bond version."

It took him a moment, but Rex put it together. "Your granny was KGB?"

Nadia nodded. "But Nana Tania played both sides of the iron curtain. She came to despise the ugly reality of the Soviet Union and began selling secrets to the Americans and British. She got caught, then escaped two days before her execution date. Her friends smuggled her and my mother out of the country, and they wound up here."

Rex could only imagine what such a journey had entailed. "Sounds like she was one tough broad."

"She was scary. She killed her first man when she was twelve. A German soldier who tried to rape her. Killing isn't something I admire, but I understand the necessity of it in certain circumstances."

Rex nearly fell out of his chair.

Nadia smiled faintly. "You thought you were going to shock me, and now I've shocked you."

He couldn't deny it. But beyond his surprise was a grudging respect for this woman who was such a study in contradictions. So feminine and fragile looking, like a ballet dancer, but a Ph.D. superscientist who worked on top secret projects. A woman who obviously was afraid of her abusive ex-husband, but who faced that fear and was doing her best to conquer it. A young mother dedicated to her daughter, yet familiar with the depravities of the human mind and not uncomfortable with them.

He'd never met anyone like her.

"So if your history as a sniper is the skeleton in your closet, don't worry. I consider it an advantage."

"Only because you still don't know the whole story." He took a deep breath, needed to get it all out in the open. "I had a meltdown, a mission that went bad. People died because of my mistake. One day I just couldn't do my job. The Marines cut me loose."

"I don't think that's so uncommon. Did you get help?"

He knew she meant counseling. "Three months in the psych ward at Bethesda."

"It must have helped. You seem perfectly healthy to me. You're carrying on."

He shrugged. "I was lucky I had a job waiting for me at First Strike. A lot of guys in my position don't have any support waiting for them when they come home. But 'perfectly healthy' might be stretching it."

"So what *is* the problem?" she said, cutting to the heart of the matter. He admired her directness.

He returned the favor. "I don't know if I could kill again, no matter what the circumstances."

She looked at him sharply. "Then you're in an odd profession."

"I'm particular about the cases I take on," he explained. "Usually I don't do kidnappings or any kind of hostage situation. Going up against a bad guy, risking my own life, that's one thing. But I don't want to be responsible for anyone else getting killed because I hesitate or wig out or whatever."

"So you couldn't shoot someone, even to save an innocent life?"

"I don't know. I'd like to think I could, but I just don't know." It was something he'd never admitted to another living soul, not even Ace or his sister. But Nadia deserved to know what she'd gotten herself into by choosing him. "I'll completely understand if you'd like to hire someone else for this job. Beau and Gavin, both ex-cops—totally competent. Either one would be a good choice. Ace, too."

"And Lori?"

He rolled his eyes. "You don't want to hire Lori."

"I saw her in action. Pretty impressive." She started to smile, then sobered. It was easy, Rex knew, to forget for a second or two when you were in the middle of a crisis. A moment of humor, a smile. Then you remembered that you were caught behind enemy lines getting shot at, or in a field hospital waiting for a buddy in surgery, and the smile died and you felt guilty as hell for forgetting, even for a moment.

"I don't want to hire anyone else," she said. "For whatever reason, I trust you. I believe you'll do what needs to be done when the time comes."

Her belief in him was surprising, to say the least. She had no evidence to support that confidence—but he supposed that was what defined faith.

"If you're sure…"

She put a hand on his arm, and it felt abnormally hot to him, as if she'd had her hands warming near a fireplace. "I'm sure."

He felt the light physical contact all the way down to his toes—and points in-between. *Not the time for that nonsense,* he told himself sternly. "I'll try not to disappoint you."

She pulled her hand away and the moment passed. A few minutes later they were clearing the table, rinsing dishes, loading the dishwasher. Nadia pulled a clean cloth wipe from a dispenser and attacked the laminate top of the table with a vengeance, then did the same with all the countertops and the sink.

"I can't help but notice you're very…tidy," Rex observed.

"What, because of this?" She held the wipe up, then tossed it into the trash compactor. "I'm a biochemist. All day long I look at viruses and bacteria. I *know* what lurks on dirty countertops, and I can't stand it."

"You'll never get them all, you know."

She blushed. "I know. But I can't help myself."

"I can just imagine what you thought of the First Strike office," he said as he hung up the dish towel he'd been using to dry the soup pan after washing it.

She promptly whipped the towel off the rack and took it to the laundry room, then got out a fresh one. "I'm surprised there aren't terrorists standing in line at your door, wanting to collect specimens to cultivate for germ warfare."

"We have a certain image to protect." He flexed his muscles. "Tough guys don't let a few germs bother them."

Nadia didn't crack a smile. "If you had any idea—" She stopped there.

THE PACKAGE ARRIVED just before ten o'clock that night.

It had been a long and rather tedious afternoon and evening for Nadia. Rex had tried to get her to relax. His best guess had been that Peter would take it to the wire, waiting until the last possible moment to deliver the videotape, if he delivered it at all. Peter was playing a psychological game with Nadia, and showing any eagerness to operate under her rules would give her more power.

If she'd known that, she would have set the deadline earlier. As it was, they had the evening, tonight, and all day tomorrow to play the waiting game. And all the while, God knew what was happening with Lily.

Nadia tried to watch TV, but she couldn't concentrate enough to follow even the simplest sitcom plot. She tried to read but encountered the same problems. To pass the time, she built a small blaze in her fireplace. The weather had been mild for January, but still cool enough that the warmth of a fire was welcome. Rex, meanwhile, stalked around her house like a tiger on the prowl with Sophie at his heels, peeking through the blinds at the street, then the overgrown backyard beyond the patio, then the side yard. He went upstairs and down, then back up. His gun was always in the holster at the small of his back.

At about nine o'clock, Nadia took a pan of lasagna from the freezer and stuck it in the oven. She was not remotely hungry, but Rex might be. He was a big guy. And they both needed to keep up their strength for whatever lay ahead. When it was ready, Rex again joined her in the breakfast nook.

"I didn't think I was hungry," he said, "but this smells great. Where'd you learn to cook?"

"Mostly from cookbooks. My mother couldn't do much in the kitchen, and my grandmother was hopeless. She could boil things, but one gets tired of boiled eggs, boiled chicken, boiled cabbage."

"No kidding. Well, this is really good."

He ate quickly, then fed Sophie from a bag of food he'd brought from the First Strike office.

They said little as the waiting took a toll on their nerves.

"You want ice cream?" she asked suddenly. "I have rocky road. And butter pecan."

"Sure, I'd—" Suddenly he tensed, laid a hand on her arm and put a finger to his lips. He swiveled his head slowly in all directions, listening intently.

At first she didn't know what had caused his reaction. Then she saw that Sophie had gone on the alert, ears pricked, every muscle tense. The dog jumped up and ran to the door, but didn't make a peep.

Then Nadia heard what the dog had, a truck engine. In her driveway.

Rex jumped up and sprinted to the front door to peer out the fish-eye peephole.

"Quickstep Delivery," he said. "This could be it. I'll be just around the corner with Sophie. Open the door wide and scream if anything seems out of the ordinary."

She nodded, wiped her suddenly damp hands with her napkin, then headed for the door, anticipating the doorbell. When it rang, she waited a few seconds, taking long, deep breaths, then opened it.

"Package for you, ma'am." The delivery person was a woman, small, nonthreatening. With the door open wide, Nadia signed for the package, which was small and wrapped in brown paper—just large enough to hold a videotape.

The woman handed the box to Nadia and sprinted off. Nadia closed the door. She wanted to rip into the package with hands, fingernails, even teeth. Here, finally, was the evidence she longed for, the pictures that would prove her baby was still alive.

Or not.

"Give it to me."

She knew that was the wise thing to do. The package was potential evidence. And while fingerprints or DNA evidence weren't essential at this stage—there was no debate as to the kidnapper's identity—preserving evidence still made sense.

Rex took the package to the kitchen, where there was plenty of light, and carefully slid his penknife under the tape to remove the paper as Nadia peered around his shoulder.

When he lifted the lid on the box, it wasn't what they expected. No videotape, just some wrinkled tissue paper. Then she saw it, a flash of something red, red and sticky....

Rex must have seen it at the same time, because he shoved her back. "Don't look!"

But she wasn't about to look any closer. She was already dizzy, clutching at the edge of the granite counter to keep from tumbling to the floor.

Chapter Six

With his gut clenching, Rex delved deeper into the white tissue paper. *Oh, God, don't let it be, don't let it be.* Then he saw what it was, and said a silent prayer of thanks.

"It's not blood," Rex said quickly. He turned his attention from the box to her, grasping her by the arms to keep her from collapsing. "Nadia, it's okay, it's nothing, just a sick joke."

Finally he got through to her. She looked up at him, her eyes moist with tears. "Not blood?"

"No." He enfolded her into his arms and let her gasp against his shoulder. She wasn't crying, exactly, just getting air into her lungs, a strange loss of control resulting from intense relief. He'd known this moment would come sooner or later. She'd been holding herself together for a very long time, and it was never a question of if, but when, she would break down.

Her arms slid around him, and he tried not to think about how good it felt to just hold her. The top of her head didn't even reach his chin, she was so tiny, and she felt fragile as a little bird. He let himself stroke her curly hair, which felt soft as a cloud.

His groin hardened, and he could only hope she didn't notice. He would never take advantage of a woman in such a vulnerable state, but his body didn't have such a strict code of ethics.

After a moment she collected herself and pulled away. "I guess I am squeamish," she said apologetically. "I've never gone weak at the knees like that before. What is it? What's in the box?"

"I don't think you should look."

But he was too late, she was already looking. "Oh, my God."

Peter Danilov had cut off the ear of a doll, poured red syrup on it and had it delivered to Nadia.

"He is so sick," Nadia said, shoving the box away.

"He's just trying to unnerve you."

"Well, he succeeded."

"He got the reaction he wanted," Rex agreed. "The important thing is not to let him know he succeeded. This doesn't mean he won't still deliver the video. But he's not going to do it meekly."

"What do we do now?" Nadia asked.

"We wait. My guess is he'll—" the phone rang "—call," Rex finished.

They checked the caller ID, which told them the call was anonymous. Nadia looked up at him with wide-eyed apprehension. "It's him. What do I say?"

"Just don't let him know he upset you. Remember, be strong. You're in control of what Peter wants. You make the demands."

The cordless phone rang again, loud and shrill in the cavernous kitchen. With a shaking hand, Nadia picked it up and hit the talk button. Rex leaned close so he could hear the other end of the conversation. Her hair tickled his cheek, the almond scent of her shampoo teasing him, reminding him of a burgeoning desire that he did not want.

"Hello," she said, her voice surprisingly strong, sure.

"Did you get my present?" Peter asked, his voice silky.

"Since you seem to have time to play sick games," Nadia said coolly, "I'll make it more challenging. You have until noon tomorrow to deliver the video. Not midnight. Noon. Or it's the CIA."

"You can't—"

Nadia hung up on him.

Rex squeezed her shoulder. "Damn, you're good."

His praise seemed to please her. She smiled tremulously. "Did I do the right thing? I just didn't think I could stand waiting another whole day. I have to know Lily's all right."

"You did the right thing." They were still standing very close, the phone clutched in Nadia's hand between them. Rex took the phone from her cold hand and set it on the base.

They both jumped when another phone rang. Rex pulled his consciousness away from Nadia and dug his cell phone from its tiny holster on his belt.

"Yeah," he growled into the phone.

"Back at ya." It was Lori.

Rex took a deep breath. "Sorry, sis, what do you have?" Lori could hack into the phone company at will. He remembered that last year she'd dated a telecom engineer. He wondered whether she'd really liked him that much, or she just wanted information from him.

"Was it him?" she asked.

"Yeah."

"He was calling from another pay phone, outside the Crestmont Shopping Center. If we staked out every damn pay phone in the city, we'd have him. As it is—"

"He'd be gone before we could get there," Rex finished for her. "Same story as earlier. Map out the sites and maybe we can triangulate where he's coming from, anyway."

"Right. What did he want?"

"Just to rattle Nadia's cage. But a word of warning, Lori, and you can pass this on to the other guys. Peter Danilov is one sick puppy. If it comes to a showdown, don't underestimate him. He's capable of anything, absolutely anything."

He ended the call, then returned his attention to Nadia. "Not good news?" she asked.

"He was using another pay phone. In Crestmont."

"That's near where my grandmother lived. There's a pretty large immigrant population in that neighborhood. I'll bet it's not far from where Peter's staying."

"His comfort zone," Rex said. "Someplace where his accent won't make him stand out. But he won't use that phone again. He likes to mix it up."

"You've come to understand him very quickly."

"I know his kind. He's cocky and he's a bully. He's intelligent. So long as he has the upper hand, he's a formidable enemy. But I think he'll crumble when he realizes just who he's up against."

"I'd like to see the two of you in a fight," Nadia said, nodding appreciatively. "I know who'd win."

"I was talking about you," he said gently. "You're the formidable enemy. I'm just the coach."

She shook her head. "I'm not strong."

He took both of her hands between his and rubbed them. She had felt so warm to him earlier, but now she was freezing. "You've stood up to him, and that takes real courage."

Her voice dropped to a whisper. "But I'm so scared. I'm so scared, Rex. What if he sends a real ear the next time? What if he hurts my baby?"

"I'll tear him apart." Brave words, coming from a man who earlier in the day declared he didn't know if he could muster the gumption to kill someone no matter what the circumstances.

But it was what Nadia needed to hear. She reached up and touched his face. "Thank you."

He moved into her light caress the way a dog does, craving her touch. And before he knew what was happening their lips met. Fueled by tension and pent-up feelings, the kiss was not gentle, but Rex didn't think Nadia wanted gentle. She battled as fiercely as he did, lips and teeth and tongue waging passionate war, breaking contact briefly for a gasp of oxygen, enough to keep the brain functioning, then together again. Her hands touched him everywhere, his somehow got tangled in that wonderful cloud of hair.

He didn't know how the kiss had started, or how he'd let it get so out of hand. With Nadia invading his senses, every sane thought flew from his brain like a flock of crazed chickens fleeing a butcher. The only thing he did know was that he never wanted it to end.

But it had to end. "Nadia…" he murmured against her mouth.

"Please," she said on an anguished groan. "Please don't let go of me. If you stop touching me, the fear will crush me like an insect."

"You're going to be fine," he crooned, stroking her hair, trying to defuse the explosive situation. Tenderness, not passion, was what a frightened woman should have.

"I think I'm going to die."

He recognized a full-blown anxiety attack when he saw one. He used to have them himself. Though it had been years, he always kept a current prescription of diazepam in his duffel—just in case. He should get one of the potent little pills for Nadia—Lord knew she could use an antianxiety drug. But the moment he opened his mouth to suggest it, she kissed him with renewed passion. And though he was twice her size, he was helpless to resist. His own desires had been whipped up into such a frenzy, they threatened to consume him.

"You must think I'm crazy," Nadia said when she came up for air.

"I know you're making me crazy," he said before he could think of a more appropriate rejoinder. Then, clearing his senses slightly, he added, "I don't think you're crazy. I think you're beautiful and smart and brave, and you're overcome with emotions."

"Why am I doing this?" she asked on the verge of tears. "Why do I need this now? I swear I'm going to die."

He understood exactly what was going on with her.

He'd seen soldiers in prebattle situations. In times of extreme life-or-death stress, emotion found an outlet where it could—sex, violence, uncontrollable weeping. Given the other choices, sex wasn't such a bad idea.

Still, he wasn't comfortable with it. Though at this point his hormones threatened complete domination over his brain, he still had some semblance of conscience left. He couldn't take advantage of Nadia. It was possible that she might eventually forgive him, but he could never forgive himself.

"Stop thinking," she said, sliding her hands under his T-shirt. He shuddered at the feel of her soft hands against bare skin.

"Nadia…"

Without warning she withdrew her hands and pulled her sweatshirt over her head, revealing a lacy white bra. His gaze fixed on her breasts, full and golden, straining against the lace as if aching for his touch.

He looked back at her face, and whatever objection had been forming died in his throat. She didn't want to beg, but somehow he knew she would if she had to.

He stopped resisting, knowing there was no point. He wanted her as much as she did him, and she wouldn't be leading this charge if she didn't know how to handle it, he reasoned. She wasn't some sheltered virgin.

Decision made, there were no holds barred now. Rex pushed her up against the refrigerator and kissed her hard, which only seemed to inflame her further. While he worked the front clasp of her bra, she squeezed his butt, then slid her hands around to his zipper to flirt with the obvious hardness there.

His hands shaking, his concentration shot by her bold caresses, he had to admit defeat with the damned bra. She pushed his hands aside and took it off herself. Then she was standing in front of him in only her jeans and socks, bare from the waist up, her breasts smooth and golden with only the hint of last summer's tan lines from a very brief bikini.

The glare of the kitchen lights seemed all the harsher shining on Nadia's softness. "Not here," he said, eyeing the tile floor and granite counters. Nadia needed softness around her.

She nodded somberly, took his hand and led him without a word through the kitchen and into the entrance hall. Sophie, snoozing on the carpet near the door, opened her eyes briefly to make sure this new activity didn't concern her, then closed them again.

Rex had thought Nadia was heading for the master bedroom, but instead she veered off to the darkened living room, to a white, faux-fur rug near the fireplace.

It was the perfect backdrop.

With uncommon efficiency they worked together to peel off Nadia's jeans, panties and socks. His clothes followed. He didn't try to slow things down. He knew what she needed now—she needed it fast and emphatic. Frankly, at this point, he wasn't in the mood for slow, longing looks and lingering caresses. He wanted to possess her, to exorcise her demons with the heat of his sex.

She looked amazing in the firelight, her hair cascading around her shoulders and down, the curls teasing the rosy tips of her breasts.

Following his instincts, he leaned down and took

one nipple in his mouth. She tasted sweet, and he swirled his tongue in circles, rewarded by Nadia's low groan of pleasure.

She clung to him, unable to hold herself up, and they more or less fell to their knees, then all the way down onto the pillowy rug. He kissed the other breast, kneading both and raking the nipples with his teeth as Nadia writhed and gasped and dug her fingernails into his back.

He needed no further foreplay, but he didn't want to hurt Nadia by overestimating her eagerness. He reached between her legs and stroked her soft folds, and she opened for him like a flower dripping nectar.

"Now, Rex, please, I can't stand it anymore."

He needed no further coaxing. But he did need protection. He should have thought of that before. "I'll be right back."

By some miracle, he found a condom in an inside pocket of his jacket. When he returned to Nadia, she still had her eyes closed, waiting, perfectly trusting. Amazing.

He lay back down beside her and took care of the protection. Then he returned his attention to his beautiful flower.

"You're sure?"

She groaned something that sounded like a yes, and he plunged inside her, sheathing himself to the hilt, and those fingernails dug into his shoulders again as she took him.

With each thrust she rose up to meet him, counter-thrusting almost as hard as he did. He was still afraid of hurting her, she was so small, but she did not seem bothered by his lack of finesse.

He didn't last long. Even if he kept his eyes closed, he intuitively saw her—her wild, tangled hair the color of dark chocolate, her lips moist and red as if she'd been eating cherries, her dark eyes glazed with passion. Her image was etched into his brain—at that moment, he believed it would be the last thing he ever could forget.

He held on until he felt her tighten around him. When she found her release, she screamed loud enough to break glass and he cried out words of encouragement and meaningless endearments until he, too, shook the house with the intensity of his peak.

When the real world came back into focus, Nadia was weeping. Rex quickly withdrew from her, hoping like hell he'd done the right thing by giving in to her slightly mad seduction. What if he'd just made everything worse?

But maybe she was just crying from her climax. It was a common physiological reaction and might have little to do with her current state of emotions. He gathered her against him and just held her while she wept.

She quieted after a few minutes, but she made no move to pull away. He could have held her like this forever, with the dying fire casting a red, unearthly glow over the whole room, as if they were in a cocoon where no one and nothing could touch them.

But reality intruded soon enough.

"You must think I'm insane, a monster, to want to have sex with a man I barely know when my daughter's been kidnapped by a maniac."

"I don't think anything like that. It's normal." And he told her about his previous experiences in life-or-death stress situations, and how she needed a safe outlet for her emotions. He thought she was somewhat comforted by his words.

"It's not very fair to you, though," she said. "You must feel used."

"When was the last time you heard a guy complain about that?" he teased.

"Well, at any rate, I want you to know that it wasn't just because you were available and had the right equipment. I would never have done that with just anyone. In fact, I've never—well, not since Peter, anyway."

"You don't owe me any explanations, Nadia."

"But I need to say it. It's true I don't know a lot about you, but I know most of the stuff that counts. You're smart and you're kind and incredibly gentle—"

"Gentle?" That was a word he'd never heard applied to him. Ex-sniper bounty hunters weren't usually described in those terms.

"Yes," she insisted. "You would never hurt me, or anyone innocent. I know that about you as surely as I know the color of your eyes."

She was right about that, anyway. In only a few hours he'd come to feel incredibly protective toward her. But he'd always been a bit of a sucker when it came to defenseless women. That was part of what had ended his military career.

"You should know something about me, though," Nadia continued. "It can't be anything more than the here and now for me. Not that you'd be interested, but just in case."

It took him a few moments to assimilate what she meant. "You mean you can't get involved."

"Yes, that's what I mean."

Rex should have felt relieved. Usually he was the one who made that speech. He'd learned through painful trial and error that he wasn't destined for a long-term relationship. Men like him didn't mix well with normalcy—dating, meeting parents, remembering birthdays, going to company Christmas parties. Those few women he'd hooked up with who weren't totally freaked out by his history quickly tired of the other garbage they had to put up with. His schedule was unpredictable, and he often picked up with no notice at all and would be gone for weeks. Then there was the fact that he never knew when some jerk he'd dragged into custody might get paroled and come gunning for him.

Most women didn't like sleeping with a loaded gun always within reach. Most women couldn't tolerate a man who wouldn't sleep through the night, either.

But having Nadia beat him to the punch—well, it wasn't good for his ego, he supposed.

"I don't do relationships," he said. "You're safe."

"Really? Why not?" She propped herself up on one elbow and absently toyed with his chest hair. Then she ran her finger over the bandage that covered his most recent injury. She looked a damn sight better than she had before they'd had sex.

"You first."

"I know what you're thinking," she said. "That after Peter, I think all men are jerks, once bitten, twice shy and all that."

"That's not the case?"

"I know there are good men in the world. My father was one. Here's the thing, though. Any two-bit terrorist can do what Peter's done—blackmail me by threatening the person I love. Even if I didn't have physical access to dangerous technology, I have things in my head that should never be shared. The more people I have in my life, the more vulnerable I am."

"You can't go through life—"

"Lily is everything I need," she said softly.

God, no wonder she was so panicked at the thought of anything happening to her daughter. Not that any mother wouldn't be, but Lily was everything she had—*everything*.

They were silent for a while as reality reestablished itself around them—the reality that Lily was absent. Then Nadia said, "Your turn."

After Nadia's confession, he couldn't very well blow her off now. "Bounty hunters don't make good boyfriends," he said, simplifying his explanation.

"You could do something else."

"So could you. You don't have to work in top-secret research."

"Touché. You love your work?"

"It keeps me busy." He paused, realizing she deserved a less flippant answer. "I honestly don't know what else I would do."

"Same here."

That pretty much negated any possibility of this going anywhere. And he didn't want it to, Rex reminded himself. He had no business feeling even the tiniest disappointment.

But he did.

NADIA STILL COULD NOT believe she'd done what she'd done. Even if there was a logical explanation for it, she felt guilty for focusing on something so trivial-seeming as sex while Lily was missing and in danger. Now, in addition to worrying about her daughter, she had to deal with the awkwardness of ending this interlude and moving forward as if nothing had happened.

She eased away from Rex and looked at his bandaged arm again. "How is your arm? I should have been more considerate. I might have hurt—"

"My arm is fine. Why don't you take a long, warm shower?" He sat up and smoothed Nadia's hair across her shoulder in a caress that was anything but awkward. "It'll help you sleep."

"I don't think I'll be able to sleep."

"It would be good if you could." He pushed up to his feet in one graceful move, totally unself-conscious about his nudity. He was a gorgeous man, all firm muscle and sinew, not an ounce of anything soft on him. The red glow from the dying fire cast intriguing shadows across the hard, flat plains of his musculature. He seemed to be tan all over, though the taut skin of his buttocks was slightly more pale than the rest of him.

When he offered her his hand, she used it to pull herself up, wishing she had a robe handy. This was one situation with which she was totally unfamiliar. She'd never been very adventurous where sex was concerned, and she'd always had at least some bedcovers she could hide under when feeling shy.

To his credit, Rex didn't stare, nor did he make a point of averting his gaze. He seemed comfortable.

Taking a deep breath, she raised up on her tiptoes and gave him a quick kiss on the cheek in gratitude.

"What was that for?" he asked.

"For taking care of me."

"I wasn't exactly ignoring my own needs," he said, looking down at his feet.

"You did precisely what needed to be done—and you didn't judge me for it. For that, I thank you." Then she darted for her bedroom and took a very long shower.

PETER HAD FOUND A SPOT on a street one block away, on the side of a hill, from which he had a good view of Nadia's house. He'd been watching for an hour, now, long enough to know she was home. The curtains and blinds were all drawn, so he had no hope of actually seeing inside. But he'd been watching lights go on and off.

He'd also seen the huge, black dog come out the back door, do its business, then return inside. Since when had Nadia gotten a dog? For protection? Against him, perhaps?

He shook his head at her foolishness. A guard dog was no match for a bullet.

He saw the bathroom light go off. At almost the same instant, the kitchen light went on. And suddenly he was no longer amused as he was reminded of the fact that

Nadia wasn't alone. He'd told her to ditch the bounty hunter, and she had refused. She'd refused! He had her daughter. She should be desperate to follow his orders. What was wrong with her?

He'd wanted Nadia alone, isolated, where he could prey on her worst fears and she would have no one to console her. But she wasn't alone. That bounty hunter was coaching her to defy him. She'd never talked back to him before, never made demands. When he caught up with the bounty hunter, Peter thought with a grin, he'd kill him. And he'd make Nadia watch.

Chapter Seven

When Nadia emerged from the bathroom wrapped in her favorite, raggedy terry robe, the bedroom was empty. Feeling suddenly anxious, she hurried out to the hallway and down to the living room. "Rex?"

"In the kitchen," he answered back. Wearing a pair of sweatpants and a long-sleeved U.S. Marines T-shirt, he poured milk into a saucepan on the stove. Sophie, who was the most well-behaved dog Nadia had ever encountered, lay at Rex's feet. The box Peter had sent and its pseudogrisly contents were gone.

"How're you doing?" Rex asked.

"Better, I guess." The panic that had been expanding in her gut, threatening to erupt all day, had receded somewhat. The fear was still there, but Nadia now felt as if she had some control over it, that it wouldn't overwhelm her and drive her completely mad. "I still don't think I'll be able to sleep."

"That's why I'm making hot chocolate."

"I think a couple of horse tranquilizers would work better."

"You wouldn't take tranquilizers even if I had them."

"How do you know that?"

"You don't like to let go of your control."

He was right, and it unnerved her that Rex could read her so accurately. She'd always insisted on having a handle on every aspect of her life, whether it was her job, her health, her home or her child. It had hit her especially hard when she'd not been able to save her beloved Nana from the ravages of the horrid disease that had taken her with such agonizing slowness. It had hit her even harder when she'd realized her marriage was a complete sham and she had no power to fix it.

"It seems wrong to sleep while my baby is out there somewhere," she said. Then again, it had seemed wrong to have sex, and she'd done that. Her face burned at the sudden reminder.

"You have to sleep. Tomorrow, when things start happening, I'll need you at a hundred percent."

"I'll try."

She sat with Rex in the breakfast nook and sipped at the hot chocolate. She wanted to look out the blinds and reassure herself that Peter wasn't on her patio. She kept imagining him lurking out there, ready to crash through a window and snatch her away. But Rex had cautioned her to keep the blinds closed. Sophie would know the instant anyone came close.

"Do you want to sleep in my bed tonight?" she asked.

Rex looked slightly startled by the question, but Nadia wanted to know, and she wasn't the type to mince words.

"Oh, yeah. I want to. But only if you'd feel comfortable."

"I'd feel safer." She'd never been afraid to be alone.

She'd been a loner as a kid, a brainy nerd with her nose buried in science books, and it had never bothered her. Even after the jaw-breaking incident with Peter, she hadn't felt afraid, exactly. She'd become extracautious about her personal safety, a bit anxious on occasion, but her precautions had given her a false sense of security.

Now she felt afraid to be alone. Even in the shower, she'd had a moment or two of unease.

"Then I'll stay with you."

Okay, that was settled. In an uncomfortably businesslike fashion, she admitted. Granted, she was the one who'd made it very clear that she was not up for anything beyond a quickie night of passion. But the night wasn't over by several hours, and she wouldn't have minded hiding away in a comforting cocoon of counterfeit intimacy, at least until sunrise.

But Rex had been accommodating enough. She couldn't possibly ask for anything more from him. He probably already thought she was a needy sex fiend.

"Do you want more?" he asked, nodding toward her almost-empty mug.

She shook her head and stood, taking both their mugs to the sink. Rex just shook his head as she scrubbed them both, put them in the dishwasher, added soap and turned it on.

"You don't even wait until it's full to run it?"

"I run it every night. I can't stand the thought of those dirty dishes getting germier by the minute while I sleep."

"But they're not dirty. You scrubbed them sterile before you even put them in the dishwasher."

"We're not going to agree on this."

He smiled. "No, I guess we're not." He held out his hand to her, and she took it. They walked together, hand in hand, to the bedroom.

"You'll be all right while I take a shower?" he asked.

"Sure. Sophie will guard me."

"I'll leave the bathroom door open. Just yell if you need me."

While Rex was showering, Nadia took off her robe and crawled under the covers. It was after midnight, and she'd gotten almost no sleep the previous night at the hotel. Two days ago, her life had been incredibly normal—cleaning house, giving Lily a bath, shopping. Shopping. If only she'd put that off…but no, Peter would have gotten to her somehow.

She let her thoughts drift toward Lily, picturing her soft, curly hair, her rosebud mouth, her incredibly dark brown eyes. What if she never saw her baby again? What if someday she forgot what Lily looked like, what she smelled like, what it felt like to hold her warm little body in her arms?

Rex emerged after a very quick shower with a towel wrapped around his lean hips. He took the clothes he'd been wearing and tucked them into his duffel.

"I sprayed that stuff on your shower door so it wouldn't get soap scum."

"I'm not a freak. You can leave any kind of mess you want. You can even leave dirty towels on the floor. I won't say a thing."

"You'll just quietly clean up after me. No, we're not going there. I'll just hang this up now." He stepped back into the bathroom, removing his towel as he did, then returned to the bed nude. "I don't wear pajamas."

"Not a problem." Not at all. She'd have been disappointed if he'd climbed into bed wearing anything as pedestrian as pajamas. Didn't suit his image.

He turned out the lights, told Sophie to patrol the house and climbed under the covers. "Do you want me to stay on my side of the bed?"

"No."

"Good." He slid an arm under her shoulders and pulled her close, nestling her against his chest.

She inhaled deeply and realized he'd bathed with her girly-smelling shower gel. On him, though, it didn't smell girly, just clean and citrusy and—oh, she didn't want her thoughts going there.

"Just a warning," he said. "I can't hold you like this and not get aroused. You probably noticed."

No, she'd been too busy noticing her own state of arousal. "I'm sorry. Do you want me to—"

"I want you to sleep."

"But—"

"Sleep."

"Okay." And amazingly, she did.

NADIA STIRRED some hours later, disoriented and cold. She knew something was wrong but had a hard time figuring out what it was at first. Then she remembered. Lily was gone. And Rex was no longer in bed beside her.

She heard a noise, a sort of groan, and knew instantly that was what had awakened her. Rex! Had something happened? Had Peter gotten in, gotten past the dog and taken Rex by surprise? Was he in her bedroom, ready to pounce on her?

She'd left a light on in the hallway, which sent a sliver of light through the partially open door—enough that she could make out the shape of Rex's gun lying on the nightstand on his side of the bed.

The groaning noise came again. It was definitely in the room with her, on the floor near the other side of the bed.

Nadia crawled across the bed, grabbed the gun, pointed it toward the doorway and switched on the bedside lamp. If she saw Peter, she would shoot him.

But what she saw was Rex, naked, lying half under her bed and groping the floor, trying to pick up something that wasn't there.

She realized immediately what was happening and tossed the gun on the bed. She was by Rex's side in an instant, but she hesitated to wake him up abruptly. She'd awakened her grandmother from a nightmare once and the old woman had grasped Nadia by the throat and, with surprising strength, had very nearly strangled her unconscious before she'd come fully awake and realized what she was doing.

Nadia moved a couple of feet away. "Rex? Rex!"

"It's gone!" he cried, the first intelligible words he'd said. "Where is it?"

"Rex!" Nadia said, louder this time. Conventional wisdom said not to wake someone during a nightmare, but she couldn't just sit there and watch him suffering from what was obviously a very vivid, very upsetting dream.

His eyes opened, but she wasn't sure he saw anything other than what was in his mind's eye. "She's killed them all." He went limp, burying his face in the carpet, his shoulders heaving as he hyperventilated.

She couldn't stand it. She moved closer and touched him, gently rubbing his bare shoulder. "Rex, it's all right. You're safe."

Gradually his ragged breathing eased and he raised his head. "Nadia?"

"You were having a bad dream."

He pushed himself partway up, realizing he was stuck half under the bed. He extricated himself and sat all the way up. Nadia got a blanket and draped him with it—he was trembling with the cold. Her thermostat automatically kicked the temperature down during the night while she slept, then raised it just before her usual waking time.

She sat back down beside him and took one of his hands in hers, rubbing it gently. "You'll be fine. Just take your time, get your bearings."

"I'm sorry," he said after she'd sat with him for a good five minutes. "I haven't had one of those dreams in a long time. I thought I was done with all that."

"Post-traumatic stress disorder?" she asked.

He neither confirmed nor denied.

"I know what it looks like," she said. "My grandmother had it. It was a lifetime thing with her. Sometimes she went years without incident, then something would kick it into gear—a news report, a certain face, even the sound of firecrackers. It got much worse toward the end of her life. I can't tell you how many times I picked her up off the floor in the middle of the night. She almost killed me once," Nadia added matter-of-factly. "She thought I was a soldier trying to rape her."

"You took care of her?"

"Yes, all through high school. My mother worked nights, so I watched Nana Tania. She died the summer before I went to college."

"Where is your mother now?"

"In Michigan, still. I've tried to get her to move down here with me, but she refuses. She said she can't stand the heat."

"Your father?"

"He died when I was a child. I don't remember much about him, but my mother told me of him. He was much older than her, a gentle bear of a man." Nadia sensed her prattle was calming to Rex, so she continued. "I remember riding on his shoulders. I remember him slipping me Brach's caramels when he thought Mama wasn't looking. That's about it, but I have a few pictures. He worked at a meatpacking plant."

"My mom died when I was young," he said. "The memories are so vague."

"Do you want to get back into bed now?" she asked. "It would be warmer."

"Actually, what I want is to take a look around, make sure everything is okay. Then I want to raid the refrigerator. I've got the shakes."

"All right."

"I didn't mean to come here and eat you out of house and home."

She laughed, amazed that she could do so. "I have lots of food, so that's not a problem."

REX COULD NOT SHAKE the humiliation that saturated his entire being as Nadia dished up some ice cream and heated chocolate syrup in the microwave.

"Now that you know," he said, "maybe you'd like to reconsider my suggestion that you hire someone else for this job."

She looked at him, confused. In her blue chenille robe, her hair wildly mussed and her eyelids heavy from sleep, she was just about the sexiest little wood nymph he'd ever seen. "Now that I know what?" she asked.

"That I'm a nutcase."

"PTSD hardly makes you a nutcase. Given your history in the military, I'd be surprised if you didn't have it to some degree."

"Yeah, but I wigged out."

"You had a nightmare. Is that such a big deal?"

"It is when you're sleepwalking, too. Or, rather, sleepcrawling." Jeez, when he thought about Nadia finding him crawling around naked, he wanted to hide under a rock.

"Do you have any of the other symptoms?" Nadia asked. "Daytime flashbacks? Substance abuse? Inability to feel or express emotion? Depressive episodes?"

"All of the above, at one time or another. But not in a long time. The nightmares persisted the longest, but it's been at least two years since I had one."

"The circumstances may have triggered it. You said you avoided situations where you felt responsible for someone's safety. Now that I've thrust you into one, it probably acted like a trigger. It's no big deal."

She wouldn't think *no big deal* if she felt what it was like. She wasn't the only one around here who liked to be in control, and when your mind played nasty tricks on you, it was the ultimate loss of control.

"Anyway, no, I don't want to hire someone else. But if you want to quit I wouldn't blame you. I don't want to cause you any more discomfort."

Rex weighed her words. Yes, the stress from being in a protective role, possibly having to depend on his ability to use deadly force, was probably the catalyst for his flashback, and he hated flashbacks. On the other hand, tonight he'd had one of the most mind-altering sexual experiences of his life.

It was a fair trade-off. More than fair.

"No, I won't quit. I'm going to get your daughter back."

Rex ate his ice cream with gusto and even persuaded Nadia to take a few bites. He felt better when he was done. That sick, shaky feeling was gone. Then he worried about what to do with the dish. The dishwasher was clean. If he was at home, he would just set the dirty dish in the sink until he had a chance to unload the dishwasher. But he knew damn well Nadia would be grossed out.

To his surprise, though, she took the dish from him, set it in the sink without even rinsing it, took his hand and led him back toward the bedroom.

It was almost six o'clock, and he knew he should just get up. He'd never been able to sleep after a nightmare. But Nadia had other ideas.

"Come back to bed, just for a little while," she said when he suggested he might get dressed and get on with his day. "Just until I fall back asleep."

But when he acquiesced and got back in bed, ready to endure another cuddle and another woody that could be used to reinforce concrete, Nadia dropped her robe, pulled her nightgown over her head, and climbed in beside him totally nude.

"Make love to me again," she said, her voice plaintive. "I'm not really sleepy, and I'm not ready to deal with reality, not yet, not while it's still dark out."

Rex knew making love with Nadia was dangerous. A one-off was just an interlude, a strange commingling of circumstances never to be repeated. No ties, no promises, the only way he could tolerate getting close to a woman. When he had been driving into her hot and fast and mindless, he'd been able to tell himself it was okay, it felt great, it meant nothing.

But twice was a different story. To make matters worse, when he made love to her this time, it wouldn't be fast and hard and mindless. It would be slow and drowsy, a mysterious trip up a slow river rather than a wild, out-of-control roller-coaster ride.

Denial was on the tip of his tongue. But when he looked into Nadia's huge, dark eyes, he was powerless to deny her anything. He walked around the bed until he was standing beside her and slowly slid his arms around her. He kissed her earlobe, then her neck and the edge of her jaw while his fingers traced delicate patterns on her collarbone. Finally he kissed her full on the mouth, delving into her sweetness with his tongue. She moved into the kiss, enveloping him with her warmth, her scent.

He picked her up and placed her gently on the bed, then made love to every part of her body, every soft inch, every intriguing hollow. He kissed the inside of her elbow and the graceful arch of her foot until her quiet moans became more strident. She didn't beg, but she squirmed and maneuvered, stroked and kissed until she had him as bothered as she was.

This time when he entered her, he moved with lazy languor, taking his time to appreciate the feel of her body fitted tightly around him. He rolled onto his back, taking her with him until she rode astride him, pushing him more deeply into her. He watched the play of emotions over her face and wished she would smile at him. But even in the throes of ecstasy, he knew thoughts of her missing daughter were not completely banished.

He felt her clenching around him. Her climax came more quietly this time, but apparently just as intensely. Tears of some mysterious emotion trickled down her face as the last of her soft mewls faded into the darkness.

Rex felt almost guilty deriving pleasure from her when her hurts were so deep, her fears so unfathomable. But there was no turning back now. With a couple of final deep thrusts he peaked, his climax less of an explosion and more of a deep well overflowing, starting slow but building until he thought it would go on forever.

When it was over they lay jumbled together, literally panting.

Rex was pleased when she fell back asleep. He wasn't going to sleep himself—he didn't need much, four or five hours a night was plenty. But he remained in bed, holding her, enjoying the short amount of time he had left cocooned in their newly discovered, sensual world.

It felt real, but he knew it wasn't. Life-or-death circumstances often prompted people to make intense connections that felt very real, but weren't. They weren't based on the sorts of things that made for meaningful relationships—common backgrounds, shared interests, days and weeks and months of getting to know each other. The sort of burning connection he and Nadia had made was the kind that burned hot, then burned out.

Still, it was the closest he'd come to connecting with anyone since Korea, and it saddened him to think this would probably be the last time he held her like this. If this job went the way he thought it would, things would start to move very quickly.

Nadia was just starting to stir when Sophie, who'd been sleeping in the middle of the doorway between bedroom and hallway, alerted. She jumped to her feet and raced down the hall, but she didn't bark. She'd been trained not to bark at every little noise.

"Showtime." Rex leaped out of bed and dragged on his sweats. Nadia, instantly alert, grabbed her robe and cinched it tightly around her waist. By the time they exited the bedroom and were making their way down the hallway, Sophie started barking. An instant later, the doorbell rang.

Rex hurried to the front door and looked out the peephole. "It's a little kid on a bicycle," he whispered. "A boy."

Nadia had a look. "It's my neighbor two doors down." He looked to be alone, and harmless.

Rex ducked around the corner and silently indicated Nadia should open the door.

"Hi, Mrs. Penn."

"Justin. You're up early."

He shrugged. "Sorry. But the guy said it was important."

"What guy?"

Again, the shrug. "The guy who used to live here. With you." Justin reached into his backpack and pulled out a videotape. "He gave me ten bucks to deliver this to you."

Nadia took the tape, her hand shaking. "Thank you. But, Justin, you should be more careful about talking to strange men, especially strange men offering money for anything."

"I knew who he was."

Nadia was repulsed by the idea of Peter involving yet another innocent child in his schemes. He was obviously not worried about getting caught. Justin knew him, could identify him. "My ex-husband is dangerous," she explained patiently. "Stay far away from him in the future. Okay?"

Another shrug. "Okay. I have to go now."

"All right. Thank you again, Justin." She closed the door and turned to face Rex. "You heard?"

He nodded. "Peter thinks he's very clever, but he's being foolhardy now. He's allowing us to accumulate mountains of evidence against him."

"He probably thinks if he gets caught, he'll just get deported or something."

"Oh, no. It won't be that easy."

"Then he must not believe he'll get caught."

Rex held out his hand for the videotape. Nadia was almost afraid to let him have it. At last, a tangible connection to Lily—if the tape was genuine. If it wasn't, if it was another of Peter's sick jokes, or worse…

"Maybe I should look at it alone first."

"No," Nadia said fiercely. "I want to see it. But I want to wait, just a minute or two." She held the video next to her heart. "So long as we don't look at it, Lily is still alive."

"He wouldn't have gone to this much trouble if Lily wasn't alive. Come on. Let's go look at it together. You do have a VCR somewhere, I trust."

"In the den."

A small room off the formal living room had been set up as a cozy family room, with a TV, computer, comfortable furniture and a toy box. The TV had a built-in VCR. Nadia turned on the device and started to put the tape in, then hesitated. "Rex, you have to promise me something."

"I'll try."

"If Lily isn't on this tape, alive and well, you will kick out all the stops and help me find that bastard. And you'll let me kill him."

"I can't promise you that," he said quietly. "By killing him, you would kill your own soul. I know what I'm talking about. I don't want to see you five years from now, crawling around on the floor in the middle of the night, fighting off a flashback nightmare. Now put the tape in."

She did. And after a couple of seconds of snow, she saw the front page of a newspaper. "This is today's paper," said Peter's voice. There was no attempt to disguise his identity. "And here—" the camera panned away from the paper "—is your brat."

Nadia's heart swelled and pushed itself into her

throat. It *was* Lily, sitting on a wrinkled quilt on the floor, looking bewildered. She was wearing the same clothes as two days ago, and she looked in need of a bath, but basically she looked okay.

"Wave to Mama," Peter's disembodied voice said.

"Mama?" Lily's face became suddenly animated, and she looked around wildly. "Mama?"

"She's not here," Peter said harshly. "You're never going back to her unless she changes her attitude pretty quickly."

Lily's face crumpled, and she started crying. "Mama! Mama!"

Now Nadia's heart constricted. How could anyone be so heartless? The child might not understand the exact words, but she couldn't mistake the cruel tone in her father's voice. Lily was just a baby, an innocent. Nadia reached out and touched the TV screen. "Oh, Lily."

"Since you're so fond of deadlines," Peter said, "here's one for you. By midnight tomorrow, you'll have a pristine sample of the product ready for pickup. I'll contact you then and tell you where to bring it. If you don't answer your cell phone with your complete and utter cooperation, I'll take it you don't want to see Lily again. And get rid of that damn bounty hunter! That is, unless you want to see your precious Lily carved up into sausage."

Abruptly the video ended.

Nadia squeezed her eyes closed and balled her hands into fists until her emotions were under control.

"She's alive," Rex reminded her, moving closer to her and slipping an arm around her shoulders. "Focus on that. The rest is just BS scare tactics."

"I know," she said, swallowing back tears of intense joy and fear all intermingled. "What do we do now? He knows you're here. He's been watching the house." She shivered.

"Then we have to get away from here so he can't follow our movements." He thought for a moment, then came to a decision. "Here's the plan. We leave here, and we make sure we're not followed. Then we take this video to the crime lab and have them tear it apart. I have a hunch about something. We might be able to narrow down the location where Peter is holding Lily."

Chapter Eight

At first, Nadia hadn't been too keen on Rex's plan to bring in a member of the Payton Police Department. But clearly Peter already knew she wasn't working alone, and that fact hadn't scared him off. They needed someone official to get them into the crime lab, and the only person who might qualify was Craig Cartwright, Beau's former partner.

Rex had assured Nadia that Craig was totally trustworthy. And Craig knew people at the crime lab who would be willing to put in a little overtime and keep their mouths shut.

"I've trusted you so far," Nadia told Rex. They were still sitting on the sofa in the den, the TV screen gone to blue. "And Lily's still alive. So I guess I should go on trusting you." She reached a hand toward him as if for a caress, then seemed to think better of it and pulled back.

Rex felt it, too—the pull of their intimacy. But Nadia acted as if she wanted to draw the line between last night and today, and he knew that was best. So he pretended he never saw her near slip.

"Pack a few days' clothing and whatever else you might need," he told her.

They both took very fast showers, then packed up Rex's Subaru. They left some lights in the house on timers so it would appear Nadia was still staying there. Knowing they might be under surveillance, Nadia got onto the floor of the back seat and Rex covered her up, then got behind the wheel and backed out of the garage.

"Do you really think we'll fool anyone?" Nadia asked from her cubbyhole, her voice muffled.

"Probably not. But it doesn't hurt to try. Are you sure you'll be okay for a few minutes? I don't want you to come out until we're sure we're not being tailed."

"I'm fine," Nadia said. "What will you do if you *are* being tailed?"

"I'll call Ace and have him gather the troops. Peter might follow us, but someone will be following him, too. They won't stop him—if we had him arrested now, he could clam up about Lily's whereabouts. But Beau or Gavin or Ace can tail him, try to find out where he's staying."

Ten minutes later, after a circuitous route through several deserted neighborhoods, Rex determined that he was not being followed.

"You can come out now," he said to Nadia.

Moments later her head popped up in his rearview mirror. She had her hair pulled back in a braid today and no makeup, but the sight of her, even in a mirror, still took Rex's breath away.

"I'm coming up there," she said as she wiggled between the bucket seats. "Sophie, you'll have to move."

"Good luck."

But somehow, with lots of shoving and pulling and

stern verbal commands the dog could not possibly understand, tiny Nadia managed to dislodge the Rottweiler, which had to weigh almost as much as she did, from the passenger seat. Sophie slunk into the back seat and Nadia fastened her seat belt. "Whew."

"Just yesterday you were afraid of her."

"Wary, not afraid. Anyway, she's a big puppy."

"You wouldn't say that if you saw her attack."

They headed for a Whataburger, where Craig had agreed to meet them. He hadn't arrived yet, so Rex got them some breakfast. Nadia's appetite had improved, and she downed an egg-and-cheese burrito and orange juice with no problem. She seemed far stronger than yesterday. Seeing her daughter's face had bolstered her confidence in Rex.

God, he hoped her faith wasn't misplaced.

"So tell me about this cop we're meeting," Nadia said as she cleaned up the debris from their meal. She scrubbed the table with a paper napkin, threw everything in the trash, then cleaned her hands with antibacterial gel from her purse.

"His name's Craig Cartwright," Rex answered. "He used to be Beau's partner. Basically, he's the only cop on the entire Payton police force that any of us trust. He's surrounded by incompetence at best and corruption at worst, but somehow he manages to keep himself separate from the garbage and politics and just do his job."

"So he's a detective?"

"You can ask him yourself. That's him, coming through the door."

Nadia turned to look, and Rex could tell the scientific observer in her was studying him, seeing if she could figure him out just by his appearance.

Rex had to hand it to Craig, he didn't look like a cop. Though detectives in Payton were supposed to wear ties, Craig seldom did unless he had to. He kept what he called his "throw-down tie" in his pocket. If he spotted someone who would care, he could quickly put it on. But most of the time, like today, he wandered around in an open-collar shirt, khakis and cowboy boots. His hair was longer than regulation, too, dark blond and almost curly—the kind women wanted to touch. With his tall, rangy build, lean face and matinee-idol eyes, he never lacked for female companionship. The narrow scar that ran from his eyebrow to the corner of his mouth—acquired in a knife fight when he was a teenager—only added to his mystique.

Or that was what Lori said. Rex's sister had a crush on Craig, but she would walk barefoot on hot coals before admitting it.

Craig's gaze roved among the tables until it settled on Rex and Nadia. He nodded at Rex and ambled over. He never seemed in a hurry, but Rex knew the guy could move fast when he had to.

Always the ladies' man, he went straight for Nadia and stuck out his hand. "Craig Cartwright."

"Nadia Penn," she said, grasping his hand and squeezing it briefly. "Thank you for meeting with us. I assume Rex told you what was going on?"

"Actually, I left that for you," Rex said. He would let Nadia tell as much or as little as she felt comfortable with.

Craig pulled up a chair, and Nadia succinctly encapsulated the events of the last couple of days. "Rex tells me you're a detective," she said, as if interviewing a prospective employee. "What kinds of cases do you investigate?"

"I'm on the major crimes squad. Rape, murder, kidnapping, armed robbery. I understand you have some evidence you want me to have analyzed on the QT?"

"Is that okay?" Nadia asked. "You understand why I don't want it to be official, right? I don't want to be paranoid, but Peter may have friends on the force who would tell him if the police initiated an official investigation into Lily's kidnapping."

"I understand, and it's okay. What do you have?"

"A videotape," Rex answered. He drained the last of his coffee. "It's time-stamped, but I don't know how accurate the camera's internal clock might have been. But there's a clock in the background of the video—maybe you can enhance the picture and we can nail down the time."

"Why is the exact time important?" Craig wanted to know.

Rex was slightly hesitant to voice his theory. This type of analysis wasn't his specialty. He was trained to lie, to wait, to shoot—not to put together puzzle pieces. But he had noticed something in the video that he thought might be useful.

"The video was taken in a living room of some kind, and there's a window," he finally said after deciding it made no sense for him to hold back. Craig would tell him if he was off base. "I noticed the sound of an emergency siren in the background noise—and the very slightest reflection from a flashing red light on the window curtains."

"Really?" Nadia said. "I didn't even catch that."

"I imagine you were more focused on watching Lily. But here's the deal. If we could nail down the exact time the video was shot, then compared it to when various emergency vehicles were dispatched, maybe we could narrow down the location."

"That's a fantastic idea!" Nadia turned to Craig. "Is it possible? Or are there too many police cars and fire trucks running around the city at any given time?" That was exactly the concern Rex had, but Craig was nodding.

"It might be possible," he said. "Let's go to the lab and see what we can come up with. Then I can check with dispatch."

THE PAYTON POLICE shared a crime lab with the county sheriff's department, and it didn't look very impressive from the outside. The one-story cinder-block building sat on an obscure street in a mostly industrial area of downtown Payton, and it bore no sign to identify its function.

Craig Cartwright took Rex and Nadia through a side door and into a dingy corridor with yellowed linoleum floors and dull gray walls. So far, Nadia wasn't terribly impressed.

"I've never even been in here before," Rex said. "What kinds of testing can you do here?"

"You'd be surprised. Fingerprints, of course. Ballistics. Trace evidence analysis—hairs, fibers, stains, glass, paint."

"DNA?" Nadia asked.

"Not yet. We still have to send our samples to the state crime lab in Dallas. And the medical examiner does all the other biological stuff—they get all the tissue samples from autopsies. But we have some pretty sophisticated equipment for all the other stuff."

He paused in front of a door with a plaque that read Photographic Analysis and turned the handle.

Inside the room, which looked more like a laboratory, it was clean and bright, appearing almost sanitary. Now this was an atmosphere Nadia could understand, and she relaxed slightly. She could trust people who worked in a place like this.

A plump woman in a green sweater and black slacks sat in front of a huge video monitor. On the monitor was what appeared to be a convenience store surveillance tape, which she was examining frame by frame.

Craig paused a moment to watch her work, and Rex and Nadia stood at a respectful distance. She appeared to be totally engrossed in her task.

"Angie?" Craig said softly.

The woman jumped and turned, then smiled. "Craig. You scared me half to death."

"We made plenty of noise when we came in."

"You know how I get, though. This is from the QuikkyStore robbery last night. The guy has a tattoo on the side of his neck. I think I can bring it up."

"On his neck?" Craig repeated. "Does it look like a dragon?"

Angie peered at the screen. "Yeah, it could be."

Craig looked over her shoulder. "Oh, hell, that's exactly what it is. The perp is Sawyer Lazzaro. I've arrested that guy so many times I could recognize him easier than I could my own brother."

Angie smiled. "Thanks, Craig. You just made my day."

"Then you won't mind doing me a favor?"

"Sure, anything."

Nadia smiled inwardly. Maybe because of last night she was hyperaware of the hormonal fluctuations around her, but it was clear to her that Angie had a little thing for Craig despite the fact she wore a wedding ring.

Craig made hasty introductions. "Angie is brilliant," he said, and she beamed. "She can take the crappiest video you ever saw and pull up a gnat's eyelashes." He handed Angie the tape they'd received from Peter.

They watched it all the way through first while Craig explained Rex's theory about the time and the siren and flashing light. Though it was hard for her, Nadia focused this time on the ambient noises and the other things going on around her daughter. Sure enough, there was the very faint sound of a siren and the ghost of a flashing red light on the curtain. There was also a small, digital clock sitting on a lamp table by the sofa.

Angie froze on a frame at random. It didn't matter which one she chose, since the camera hadn't moved and the clock was in all of them. Then she blew it up to about a hundred times its original size. She pushed various buttons, which she explained were used to filter out certain hues or sharpen the edges. It only took her about five minutes to manipulate the image enough that they could read the time on the clock—11:58.

"That's within a minute of the time stamp," Rex said. "So it should be pretty accurate."

Just then the door to the lab opened and a man walked in—well, walked was an understatement. He strutted.

His neatly pressed suit, blinding white shirt and silk tie could only distract the eye so far, though—he wasn't handsome to Nadia no matter how much of a stud he thought he was. With his red hair and freckles, he reminded her of that guy on the cover of *Mad Magazine*.

A collective groan, quiet but unmistakable, rose from Rex, Craig and Angie. "Oh, hell," Craig muttered.

"Of all people to show up," Rex added under his breath.

"Angie, did you find anything?" the newcomer asked, never breaking stride. It took him a moment to realize there were other people in the room. Then he skidded to a stop, focusing on Rex. "What the hell are you doing in here? Angie, you know civilians aren't allowed in the lab." He said "civilians" in the same tone of voice he might reserve for "serial killers."

"I brought them in," Craig said. "They're witnesses."

"I have an ID on your QuikkyStore robber," Angie said quickly, distracting the redheaded man. "Sawyer Lazzaro is a repeat offender who has a similar tattoo to the one on your robber's neck."

"Lemme see."

Angie turned off the video machine. "This is Craig's case. I'm already done with yours. I just e-mailed you a blowup of the tattoo."

The man looked skeptical. "How'd you know it was this Sawyer person?"

She shrugged. "I've seen him before."

"Would you be willing to testify to that in court? That you recognize him?"

"I recognize the tattoo," she clarified, lying through

her teeth based on Craig's say-so. Nadia wondered why Craig didn't just own up to the fact he was the one who'd made the connection. "Just compare the blowup to his mug shot, and you won't need me to point out the similarity."

"We'll see." The man turned on his heel and left. No thank-you, nothing.

"Who was that rude man?" Nadia asked, and the other three laughed.

"His name's Lyle Palmer," Rex explained. "The most abrasive, obnoxious detective on the Payton force."

"Don't forget incompetent," Angie added. "I'm so sure this case will go to trial and I'll have to testify."

"Why wouldn't it?" Nadia asked.

"Because Lazzaro will plead out," said Craig. "Our district attorney never goes to trial unless it's a high-profile case that will look good on his résumé. If Lazzaro has any kind of decent attorney, he'll spend about six months in jail and be back out."

"For a chronic offender doing armed robbery?" Nadia was horrified. "If we ever catch Peter, what will happen to him? A slap on the wrist? Community service?"

"Don't worry," Rex said soothingly. "Peter will get in state or federal court. That's a different ball game."

Nadia was only slightly reassured. No wonder Payton's crime rate had skyrocketed in recent years. "I didn't vote for that guy," she said, referring to the D.A.

"I've never met anybody who did," Rex grumbled. "I think the election was fixed."

Angie was able to glean more useful information from the video. "The siren is from a fire-department ambulance," she said. "Not a ladder truck or police car. The sirens are distinctive. Also, the vehicle was moving left to right, which might tell you which side of the street the house is on."

"You are excellent, Angie." Craig gave her shoulders a squeeze and she blushed profusely. "I owe you lunch."

"Make it dinner," Angie shot back. "But don't think you can have your wicked way with me."

REX AND NADIA took Sophie out for a quick walk in the parking lot while Craig used his cell phone to call the Dispatch supervisor. Judging from the sound of his voice, he was flirting with her as he'd done with Angie. That was standard procedure with Craig—he couldn't talk to a woman without flirting, even if she'd been married for fifty years and wore support hose.

"What's his story?" Nadia asked softly. "Married? Confirmed bachelor?"

"Divorced," Rex answered. "Two preteen girls he sees on weekends. From what Beau tells me, his wife was the one who left. Fell in love with someone else. He was a dedicated family man before it happened. Still totally stuck on his kids."

"So, is he shopping for a replacement wife?"

"You mean because he flirts? I don't think so. That's just his way. He loves women. Why, are you interested?" He felt an irrational prickling of jealousy at the thought.

She sighed with exasperation. "You know I'm not. Just curious. He *is* very charming. How'd he get the scar?"

"He says he was in a knife fight when he was a kid.

Personally, I think the real story is something more mundane and he doesn't want to admit it."

By the time Sophie was done with her business, Craig was off the phone. "We're in luck. There was only one fire station ambulance dispatched anywhere near midnight last night." He consulted the small notebook he'd been writing in. "It left from the Pillar Street Station at 11:55, drove south along Dupree Street to a house in the 4800 block, where it arrived at its destination at 12:01. The ambulance didn't have its lights and siren on during the return trip."

Rex felt a sense of elation, his first real hope that they were close to nailing Peter Danilov. "So our target house will be about halfway between the Pillar Street Station and the 4800 block of Dupree."

Rex had a GPS navigation device in his car, so they all piled inside and watched while Rex brought up the appropriate map and plotted out the midpoint of the ambulance's route.

"I know that neighborhood," Nadia said. "My grandmother lived just a few blocks away. It's where a lot of Russian and Eastern Europe immigrants settled."

"That would make sense, if Peter's really connected to the Russian Mafia."

"Russian Mafia?" Craig gave a low whistle. "You didn't tell me that."

"We don't know for sure," Rex said. "But Nadia says he's loyal to the motherland and hates America, so that makes him dangerous."

"What is it he wants so bad?" Craig asked. The question was perfectly innocent. Nadia had skated around that part of the story since it didn't have a bearing on what they needed from Craig. Now the car fell silent.

It was still a sore point with Rex that Nadia wouldn't tell him what she had that Peter wanted so badly. At one time he'd had a pretty damn high security clearance. He was risking his life for her. It would be nice if he knew what was truly at stake besides Lily.

"What did I say?" Craig asked.

"I can't tell you what it is Peter wants," Nadia said apologetically, "only that it's a matter of national security—and I won't give it to him."

"Ah." Craig nodded, seemingly unbothered by the secrecy. "So, what's next? And do you need any help? I'm off the next couple of days."

"How about a door-to-door search along Dupree Street?" Nadia suggested.

"Peter isn't just going to answer the door to any yahoo who rings the bell," Rex countered. "All we would do is alert him to the fact we're closing in."

Nadia shivered. "The last thing we want to do is panic him."

"I was thinking surveillance," Rex said. "When we can narrow down the exact house he's in, we can orchestrate an extraction."

"Ugh, I think I just remembered I'm busy," Craig said. "I hate surveillance. And if anyone asks, I never heard anything about an 'extraction.'"

"That's okay, you don't have to help out on this one," Rex said easily. "Beau and Gavin are both in town this week. And Lori. We can use her Peepmobile." He watched Craig carefully from the corner of his eye. Sure enough, Craig's interest was cranked up a notch at the mention of Lori's name.

"Ah, hell, you can count me in," Craig said nonchalantly.

"I like my idea better," Nadia said. "Just sitting and watching doesn't sound very proactive to me."

"Patience pays off in this business," Rex reminded her. "I don't think you should be seen anywhere near Peter's hideaway, though. If he spots you, it'll all be over."

He could tell Nadia didn't want to agree. She wanted to be part of the operation. But in this case, he was right and she knew it. "What will I do, then? I can't go back home—he's watching."

"You can stay with Lori," Rex said. "If we give her the job of protecting you, maybe she won't want to come along with us."

"Why wouldn't you want her to do the surveillance with you?" Nadia wanted to know. "She seems more than competent to me."

"She can partner with me," Craig offered hopefully. "I'll take care of her."

Rex attempted to put it diplomatically to Nadia. "It's still early in her training. We're afraid she'll get hurt."

"Huh." Nadia folded her arms and settled into the back seat of the Subaru with Sophie. "I think you're a couple of sexist pigs, that's what I think."

Rex didn't have a reply for that. Hell, they *were* sexist. Bounty hunting was a dangerous business requiring stamina and physical strength, not to mention the intimidation factor. Rex didn't think his sister should be involved. Maybe he was old-fashioned, but he felt that men should be the ones protecting women, not the other way around.

He decided not to voice his opinion.

"Let's just go," Nadia said. "We're wasting time."

Craig followed Rex and Nadia to the First Strike office. Inside they found only Beau—running the vacuum cleaner. He looked slightly embarrassed to be caught at the domestic chore.

"Blame it on those women," he said right away.

"Lori?" Craig asked, almost eagerly. *Oh, man,* Rex thought. The attraction was obviously two-way. But Craig would be swimming upstream trying to turn Lori into a girlfriend. She was much more comfortable pretending to be a buddy, even if her hormones were running amok—as if getting romantic would make her weak, or something.

Beau laughed. "Not Lori. She has an uncanny ability to tune out the mess. I'm talking about Aubrey and Shelby. They're meeting us here for lunch, and they both get freaked if they have to wade through trash."

Rex shook his head, not really understanding the hold certain women had on certain men. Beau had gotten married last year to Aubrey Schuyler, Gavin's sister. Gavin was getting married next month to Shelby, his former parole officer. Though neither woman spent much time here, they kicked up such a fuss over the mess that all the bounty hunters had started keeping the place cleaner.

"You are so whipped," Rex said.

Beau grinned. "It's not a bad thing." Then he sobered. "Any progress?"

Rex quickly filled Beau in, then asked where Lori was.

"She went out, didn't say where."

"And you let her?" Rex demanded.

"Like I could stop her?"

"Ace hired her to do the paperwork and the computer hacking."

"Not anymore. She's started hustling up her own cases, making the rounds at the bail bond offices. You better watch out, too. She's in danger of making more money than you this month."

"Yeah, thanks to the fact she collected a bounty on Jethro Banner's bodyguard. She was supposed to stay in the car."

"Better face it, Rex," Beau said. "You're not going to contain her."

"Our dad is probably spinning in his grave. Uh, speak of the devil."

A loud, rumbling engine announced the arrival of the Peepmobile. Rex looked out the window and saw Lori hop out. She was wearing all black, trying to look like some Special Forces commando.

As soon as she entered the office, Rex saw she had a huge bruise on her cheek. "What the hell happened to you?"

"What do you mean?"

"That bruise on your face." She reached up on the wrong side first, then found the sore spot. "Oh. I guess it was the guy I just took down to the police station. He wasn't that happy to see me." She froze when she spotted Craig. "Oh, hi, Craig."

"Hi. Maybe you should have that looked at. It's pretty bad."

Lori looked at her reflection in a window and obviously didn't see anything that alarmed her, because she shrugged.

"Lori, I have a job for you," Rex said. "I need you to bodyguard Nadia. We have a lead on Peter's whereabouts. Also, can we use the Peepmobile?"

"Sure." She tossed the keys to Rex. "But I want your car in return."

"Beau," Rex said, "think you'll have time to help out with the surveillance? Maybe relieve me later tonight if we haven't caught him by then?"

"No problem."

"Hmm," Lori said. "Is it only a coincidence he asked the girl to baby-sit and the guy to go do macho things? I don't think so." But she didn't push it. A bounty hunter's freedom to run his operation his way was sacrosanct around here. No one questioned how anyone did his job, not even Ace.

"I have another job for you," Rex said to Lori. "Use the Criss-Cross Directory and find out who lives on the forty-two, forty-three and forty-four hundred blocks of Dupree Street. Even number addresses only. Give the phone numbers to Nadia and have her call each of them, see who answers, see if she recognizes either Peter's voice or the rat-faced woman's." He handed a cell phone to Nadia. "Use this to make the calls—it's untraceable."

"Where do you get an untraceable phone?" Nadia asked.

"It's best not to ask Rex too many questions," Lori said.

"Keep a list of the addresses that correspond to Russian-sounding names," Rex continued, "or where the person who answers sounds foreign. Then call me and tell me. The information might come in useful."

Rex turned to Nadia. "Keep your personal cell phone on. Check your messages at home frequently. Call me if you hear anything from Peter."

"You, too. Please, be careful. I've said it before, but don't underestimate Peter just because he's not as big or muscular as you."

"I know better." Rex liked it that Nadia worried about him. He wanted to touch her, kiss her goodbye. Turning off the intimacy was nearly impossible. But he didn't think she would welcome any overt physical affection, especially while others were watching, so he forced himself to turn and leave with Craig.

Chapter Nine

Lori drove Nadia to a place called Dudley's, which she said was a safe place to hang out because it was filled with cops. Nadia was expecting some dark, dingy, smoky bar, but it was actually very nice, all brass and polished wood and hanging baskets of plants everywhere. They got a booth in the back and ordered pasta for lunch. Though yesterday Nadia had struggled to choke down any food at all, today she was ravenous. She ate and tried not to think about the fact that Lily might be hungry or thirsty.

"Do they drive you crazy, those macho men?" Nadia asked.

"Oh, sure, but I'm used to it. As the only girl in my family and no mom, I was already used to being patronized."

"So what made you go into bounty hunting? Did you want to follow in your father's footsteps? Make First Strike a family business?"

"First Strike was actually all my idea," Lori said proudly. "Dad was a judge, and he was always complaining about the revolving door of the justice system. He would sentence bad guys to hard time and they'd be out in six months and back in front of him within a year. He felt like he wasn't doing anything. He envied his friend Ace, who was pulling bad guys off the streets right and left."

"But if the justice system is that lenient, the guys Ace pulled in probably didn't stay long behind bars, either."

"Most of the time, no. But the image of the bounty hunter, going mano a mano with the criminals, appealed to him. He wanted to face down felons when they didn't have their smirking lawyers standing next to them. He wanted to see their faces when justice caught up with them. He wanted more control."

"So he and Ace partnered up?"

"Ace didn't even have an office back then. I suggested they go corporate, print up business cards, get a Yellow Pages ad. Since Dad was a judge, his name lent some legitimacy and authority to the company. And I came up with the name, the cobra logo and the motto 'Strike first, ask questions later.'"

"And you thought you'd be a part of it from the beginning, I bet."

"Of course! I was a natural. I already had the martial arts and weapons training. I was really mad when Dad shut me out. So I signed up with the police, got halfway through the police academy when I realized they were totally sexist, too, not to mention corrupt."

"What did you do?" Nadia was fascinated.

"I tried working on my own, but that was harder than I thought. No one would hire me. I just wasn't scary enough. I went after some felons with prices on their heads, but I didn't have the resources to travel or live for weeks with no paycheck while I tracked someone. Plus, I wasn't as good as I thought I was." She laughed easily at herself, and Nadia liked that about her.

"So then what happened?"

"My dad was murdered. And the police botched the investigation so badly, and I just felt so powerless. So I went to Ace and I pleaded my case. He was ex-military police and an ex-con, and I said I wanted to find whoever killed my father and I wanted him to help me. And if he wouldn't, I would find someone who would. So he agreed to train me."

"And did you then go after your father's murderer?"

"I realized pretty quickly, after I got over the shock of losing him, that you can't chase someone who's not there. The police had no clues, no leads—or if they did, they weren't telling me. There was nothing to hunt."

Nadia sensed the story wasn't over. She continued to eat her fettuccine and, with her expectant silence, encouraged Lori to continue. It was a trick her grandmother had taught her. People abhor a conversational vacuum.

It worked. "I recently stumbled on something that might be connected, but I can't make heads or tails of it. It's a ledger book that was hidden away—something obviously important to my Dad. It's got lists of names and dollar amounts. Some of the names belong to guys who are in prison. Some of the names are dead guys."

"But not all?"

"No, not all. I've tracked down a couple of names, but the guys they belong to claim not to know my father or anything about him. Then, some of the names don't seem to exist anywhere. They're not in any phone book or database."

Nadia had to admit, the puzzle intrigued her. She'd always been good at puzzles and brainteasers, and her grandmother had taught her a lot about codes and ciphers. "I'd like to look at this ledger book some time." It would be something to occupy the left side of her brain while she waited on news of Lily.

"I have it at home," Lori said. "I'd love for a fresh pair of eyes to have a look. Are you going to eat that?"

Nadia shook her head. Although she'd been eating the rich pasta dish steadily, there was still a lot left. Lori got a to-go box for it, and soon they were in Beau's souped-up black Mustang—on loan in exchange for the Peepmobile—and headed for Lori's apartment.

Lori lived in an unremarkable one-bedroom unit in a seminew complex. Her upstairs apartment was average size, with white walls and beige carpet. The furniture was spare and utilitarian. The only thing remarkable about the living space was its lack of clutter. Lori was very tidy, but she also simply didn't have a lot of stuff— just a few books, some sports equipment like a bicycle and a punching bag, one small TV. Her kitchen was well equipped and well stocked, however, and it was all healthy food. Nadia found the apartment extremely appealing in its simplicity and lack of pretense. Lori got them each a bottle of water, then went to find the mysterious ledger book.

"If you have some blank paper, that would be good," Nadia called after her.

Lori appeared a couple of minutes later with a thick

artists' pad of manila paper, a handful of pens and the small, leather-bound book. She opened the book to the first page, which had only one word: "CANELENG."

"At first I thought it was 'Canel Engineering,' like maybe it pertained to a company Dad had an interest in. But there is no such company, and now I'm not even sure if that's a space between the *L* and the *E*."

Nadia didn't think it was. She thought it might be a jumble or a cipher, a simple code that would confuse a casual reader. As she flipped through the pages, which were in different-colored inks, she noticed that some names were highlighted in yellow, others in orange.

"The highlighting is mine," Lori said. "Yellow is for dead. Orange is for located but claims to know nothing."

The first thing Nadia noticed was that the names without highlighting far outnumbered the highlighted ones. For someone who specialized in tracking down missing persons using the latest technology, Lori had been spectacularly unsuccessful. The second thing she noticed was that there were at least two distinct forms of handwriting in this book. The entries were all printed in block letters, but there were subtle differences. The highlighted names, both yellow and orange, were in one handwriting. Most of the rest were in another.

Which means that, whatever Glenn Bettencourt had been involved in, he had at least one partner.

"There is one other thing I should tell you," Lori said. "All of the dead guys were sexual predators of one kind or another. One was a rapist. Two were sexually abusing children. My father…" Lori paused, swallowed. "My father really hated sexual predators."

Nadia immediately thought of Nana Tania, of the horror and shame she'd suffered at the hands of that long-dead soldier. She didn't have any use for rapists.

She studied the ledger book, chewing on her bottom lip. "This doesn't look good." She tapped the leather cover. "On the surface, it looks as if your father was involved in some type of criminal activity. Do you really want to know more?"

"Yes, I do," Lori answered without hesitation. "Whatever he was doing, he had a good reason for it. He was a loving father. He helped me through a very difficult time in my life. I owe it to him to find his murderer, even if I make some unpleasant discoveries along the way."

Clearly Lori had given this some thought. So Nadia sat down with the ledger book and her pad and pen. "Give me a few minutes."

"I'll need at least that long to dig up the information Rex asked for." With that, Lori disappeared into her bedroom, where her state-of-the-art computer was set up.

It took Nadia only a few minutes to determine that the highlighted names were not encoded, but the others were. Names like "Halpirr," "Novurro" and "Bohcbi," occurring one after another after another on a list, were unnatural. But the cipher was laughably easy to unravel. In less than a half hour, Nadia had the code broken and the entire list translated.

Nadia waited, not wanting to interrupt Lori's computer work. After she heard what Nadia had to say, she might not feel much like sleuthing. Nadia read a magazine on martial arts, marveling at the cool weapons anyone could buy over the Internet, and waited.

An hour after she'd started, Lori emerged with a pad of paper. "Got it," she said. "Out of almost thirty houses, only three sounded Russian—Stepanov, Kyznetsov and Ponomarev."

Nadia winced at Lori's terrible pronunciation. "And you have phone numbers?"

"Yup. But first, did you have any luck?" She nodded toward Nadia's scribblings, sitting on the coffee table.

With some trepidation, Nadia showed Lori what she'd done.

"Oh, my gosh, this is amazing!" Lori stared at the list Nadia had compiled, her eyes shining. "Do you know what this means? Look at all these leads I have now. Surely someone on this list will talk. What about that word on the first page? What does it translate to?"

"It turns out 'Caneleng' isn't in code. It's a simple anagram of your father's first name and that of his partner."

"His partner?"

Nadia explained about the two different styles of printing and how she could tell the difference. Then she showed Lori the two names: Glenn and Ace.

REX AND CRAIG SAT in the Peepmobile, parked on a side street with a lot of other cars, from where they had a good view of the entire south side of the 4300 block of Dupree Street. A good view, but not perfect. The small brick houses were jammed together like commuters on a bus during rush hour, and in certain places, trees and overgrown bushes obscured Rex's view. At least the garages were all detached, so no one could leave their house concealed as Nadia had done this morning.

Earlier they sent Craig, with a squad car and two uniformed patrolmen, to retrieve Rex's Blazer from the gun club parking lot. Now Beau was driving it. He parked on another side street and kept an eye on the next block down, just in case their main target block was too narrow.

All in all they had almost thirty houses to watch.

Rex had thought this surveillance would be a piece of cake, but thirty houses were too many for one man, and still too many for three. He was grateful for Craig's and Beau's assistance, but he still worried that Peter or Lily would slip by them. They had only pictures to go by—none of them had actually seen these people. Lori had gotten a very good look at Peter, and Nadia, of course, could recognize them all including the rat-faced woman. But Nadia and Lori were the two people they'd left back home.

At this time of day, few people were coming and going from the houses. It was a working-class neighborhood, and most of the residents were at their jobs.

"Is there a better way to do this?" Rex asked Craig, feeling the frustration. Maybe Nadia's plan to go door-to-door would work better after all.

"I thought you were the king of surveillance."

"I've never had to watch such a large target area before. And don't forget, we have a deadline. Midnight tomorrow."

"Danilov could stay burrowed in his house for that long, easily."

Rex pondered that possibility as he watched a kid on a bike coast down the street and turn into one of the driveways. The boy opened the one-car garage, stuck his bike inside and closed it again. The garage was empty of cars. Then the kid went to a side door and used a key around his neck to let himself inside.

"Latchkey kid," Rex said. "No one else inside that house." Using a diagram he'd made of the target block, he put an X through the kid's house. But he'd been able to eliminate very few houses so far.

"We'll know more later on when people start coming home from work," Craig speculated. "Any house with no activity might be suspect."

"We need more eyes and ears," Rex decided. "But Ace and Gavin are both out of town." He'd thought Gavin would be available, but he'd nabbed a last-minute job in Dallas.

"There's Lori."

Rex really hated to bring his sister into any potentially dangerous situation. Like during the Jethro Banner takedown, Lori tended to act on her own initiative.

"If I bring her over here," he said, "will you take care of her? Make sure she doesn't do anything dumb?"

"Of course." And Craig looked far too happy about the prospect, Rex thought, but he didn't have time to play guard dog.

"Then I'll let Nadia stand watch with me. She could spot her own child a lot faster than any of us could. If any action goes down, though, the ladies stay put. That's a condition of them coming along."

"Goes without saying," Craig said. But an uneasy silence followed, and Rex wondered if Craig was thinking the same thing he was—that it was damned hard to order around females like Lori and Nadia.

Rex left Craig at a corner gas station, where there was a mini-mart and a café. He could sit there for a few minutes without arousing any suspicion. After informing Beau of the change in plans, Rex headed back to Lori's apartment. He realized he was speeding and slowed down. Was he that anxious to return to Nadia? He felt uneasy being separated from her, but that was only because he was worried about her, he reassured himself.

When he knocked on the door of Lori's generic apartment, it was Nadia who answered, and she looked troubled. "I'm so glad it's you."

"What's wrong?"

"It's Lori. I'm afraid I've upset her. She pretended she was okay, but she went to take a shower and she's been in there thirty minutes with the water running."

"How did you upset her?" He tried not to sound as if he was accusing her of anything. But his protective instincts were suddenly at war. He wanted to keep both these women safe—from everything. The last thing he needed was for one to attack the other.

"I should let her tell you."

Rex strode through Lori's living room toward the bedroom and paused in front of the bathroom door. The shower was running. He knocked loudly. "Lori?"

The pipes shrieked as the water was turned off. "What? Rex, is that you?"

"You okay?"

"Of course I'm okay. Why wouldn't I be okay?" She sounded belligerent.

"Nadia said you'd tell me."

She opened the door and barreled out, followed by

a cloud of steam. She had on a surprisingly feminine pink silk robe, and her hair was wet and sticking out in all directions. "I'm fine and there's nothing to talk about."

"Okay. Whatever." He returned to the living room, where Nadia sat on the sofa all but wringing her hands. Rex would be the first to admit Lori's behavior was peculiar. She'd never been the kind of woman who threw hissy fits or cried over anything. Even when their father had been murdered, she hadn't cried, at least not publicly. But if she wanted him to know about what was bothering her, she would tell him.

"Is she okay?" Nadia asked.

"She's fine. Why do you think you upset her? She said everything's okay."

"I decoded your father's ledger book," Nadia said quietly. "It appears he might have been involved in something illegal. And that his partner in this illegal enterprise was Ace—your boss."

Rex sighed. "Oh, boy."

"She and Ace are close?"

"Yeah."

"How close?"

"Not romantically involved, if that's what you mean. Ace is more like a father figure to her, but a friend, also."

"And your friend, too," Nadia concluded.

"Yeah. Ace taught me how to shoot." Finding out Ace might be involved in his father's murder, even in some minor way, was distressing news, but now wasn't the time to deal with it. Rex had more urgent matters.

Lori reappeared shortly, dressed in her usual low-slung cargo pants and a loose, army-green T-shirt. She exchanged a look with Rex. "Nadia told you?"

"It'll be all right, sis," he said. "Whatever it is, we'll work through it."

"No," Lori said, "you'll pat me on the head and tell me not to worry about it."

"I won't, I promise. After we get Lily back, I'll look at whatever you have, and together we'll decide how to proceed. But right now, I need you a hundred percent. Can you put this thing about Ace out of your mind for a while?"

Lori straightened, looking determined. "Of course I can."

"Good. The surveillance is more complicated than I thought, and I need both of you to help. Lori, you'll partner with Craig. Nadia, you'll be with me. Lori, did you get the information I asked for?"

Lori perked up at the news that she would be included in the operation. She handed Rex a list. "Three Russian names. Nadia started with those, and then she called everyone else. No one who answered sounded Russian, but several houses didn't answer at all, not even with an answering machine. And one of them didn't have a phone."

"Which one?"

"Forty-two seventeen."

Rex remembered it instantly—a gray house in need of paint with a weedy yard and a vacant look. If it was vacant, that would explain why it had no phone. On the other hand, a vacant house would be a good place to hide out.

"Thanks, good work. Let's roll."

NADIA WAS GLAD to be moving again. She hated sitting around waiting, feeling powerless. She was surprised, though, when they stepped outside, to see that the sky had grown overcast and the temperature had dropped by ten degrees. Normally she made it a rule to watch the weather forecast, but obviously weather had fallen low on her priority list.

"A 'blue norther' is blowing in," Rex said as they trotted down the outside stairs of Lori's apartment. "Blue norther" was how Texans referred to a dramatic cold front from the north. Sure enough, the clouds on the northern horizon had taken on that characteristic bluish tinge. "It's supposed to rain some, too. Are you okay in that jacket? Lori could probably lend you something warmer."

Nadia was cold, but she didn't want to take the time to borrow a coat. "We'll be inside the van, right? I'll be fine."

"There are always extra clothes in the van if you need layers." He opened the passenger door and helped her up. During the drive back to the working-class neighborhood, he conferred briefly on his cell phone with Craig and Beau about surveillance strategy.

"My grandmother lived down that street," Nadia said as they passed Blossom Lane. "When I was a little girl, almost every family on that street was Russian or Polish or Croatian. The ladies came out of their houses every morning and swept their porches and walkways. They painted their houses pretty colors and grew flowers in boxes and pots."

"Why did so many immigrate here?" Rex asked. "Instead of to the big cities, I mean."

"I think the university offered opportunities. Many of them were highly educated but not allowed to teach in the communist countries. There's also a lot of factory work available here for the less well educated— the bottling plant just south of here, and the fertilizer plant a little farther out of town. Now the families have completely assimilated. The neighborhood doesn't have the identity it once had, and that seems sad." Newspapers blew across the unkempt patches of grass and bare dirt that passed for yards on Dupree Street.

"It certainly seems sad to me that no one keeps their yards up here," Rex said, apparently noticing the same dismal lack of pride.

Rex pulled onto a side street, turned around and parked. Nadia was disappointed when he turned off the engine. "You mean we can't keep the engine running?"

"Only if we want someone to call the cops on us."

"No, we don't want that. Okay, what do you want me to do?"

He indicated which were the target houses, touching her arm as he pointed. She was responsible for watching the five that were closest to them. Rex watched the ones farther down the block, which included the vacant house. Lori and Craig were responsible for the next block. They all had binoculars and headset walkie-talkies so they could respond quickly.

"Surveillance takes a helluva lot of patience," Rex said. "I probably should have explained to you what would be involved before I drafted you. It's dull and boring, but you can't—"

"My grandmother told me stories," Nadia interrupted. "She once hid in a barn for three days with no food and little water, waiting for someone to arrive at some farmhouse. Then she had to kill him. She said she was so hungry she stood over the dead body and ate a chicken leg."

"Good Lord. Your grandmother sounds like one interesting lady."

"She was complicated. As harrowing as the stories were that she told me, I think she saw things as a child that were so horrible she couldn't even speak of them. I don't know what happened to her parents, only that they died when she was very young. I expect it was during World War II, and that it was very bad."

Nadia flashed an unexpected smile. "I bet Nana would have hated Peter. She would have seen into his black heart. She was uncanny at reading people, and it's unfortunate I didn't inherit that same ability."

"Don't blame yourself. A good sociopath can fool anyone."

"I'm not sure he *is* a sociopath. A sociopath has no conscience, no sense of right and wrong, no interest in anything but himself. Peter cares about Russia and hates the United States. He has a moral compass, it's just incredibly skewed."

"I bet he's in this for the money."

"Let's hope we'll get the chance to find out. When we catch him, I want a crack at him before we turn him over to the authorities."

"A crack at him?" Rex repeated. "You mean with a hot light and a rubber hose?"

"No, I find bamboo under the fingernails works best." At Rex's shocked expression, she had to smile. "Don't be silly. Although the thought of breaking his jaw like he did mine has a certain appeal, I don't subscribe to torture or violence. But I would like a chance to talk to him. He has volatile emotions and a terrible temper—his one true weakness. I know how to push his buttons, and he might tell me things he would never tell a cop."

"I can't make any promises, but I'll try to honor your wishes."

She shouldn't be asking for anything, she realized. If she could just get Lily back safe and sound, she didn't care about anything else, and Rex was already doing so much. Of course, he expected to be paid for his services. But he hadn't mentioned money since their first conversation yesterday morning. Didn't most bounty hunters require some sort of down payment?

Nadia kept her gaze resolutely on the five houses that were her responsibility. She scanned them back and forth, over and over. Most people would get tired or bored by such an activity. But she knew patience, understood tedium. When she was on the brink of an exciting advance in one of her scientific projects, she never begrudged the painstaking repetition of her work. And she knew Peter and Lily were nearby—she could almost smell them. The thought that either of them might emerge from one of these houses at any time kept her on edge and alert.

"You look cold," Rex said.

Nadia realized she'd drawn her knees up to conserve body heat. She'd also unconsciously migrated slightly closer to Rex on the van's broad bench seat, perhaps drawn by *his* body heat. "I'm okay," she said.

"Well, I'm freezing. Why don't you crawl into the back and see what you can find? I can watch your houses for a couple of minutes."

Nadia pulled down the center armrest and crawled through the gap to the back of the huge van, which had been outfitted with custom storage cabinets and spaces to set up video cameras, though the cameras weren't here at the moment.

At first she only found wigs, glasses, hats and scarves. But then she hit pay dirt—a muffler, a pair of mittens, a woman's quilted jacket that had to be warmer than the light jacket Nadia wore and the pièce de résistance, a thick wool blanket.

She announced her finds to Rex as she uncovered them.

"Damn. Sure there's not a cappuccino machine back there? Hot coffee would be nice."

"No, but I found this." She held up a strange contraption. "What in the world is it?"

Rex glanced back. "It's a portable potty. Essential for a woman doing surveillance alone when she absolutely can't leave."

Ack! Nadia hadn't even considered what to do about using the restroom. But she damn sure wasn't using this thing. She put it down, got the warm clothes and the blanket and returned to her position in the front seat. Since she had the nice quilted jacket and the gloves, she gave the blanket to Rex.

"You can keep it," he said. "I'm fine."

"You just said you were freezing."

"I wouldn't be much of a gentleman if I took the only blanket."

"You never claimed to be a gentleman." And thank God for that. If he'd refused her sexual invitation last night, she'd probably be a blithering idiot by now.

"Why don't we share it?" Rex asked. The question echoed in the big van, oozing with suggestion.

Chapter Ten

Nadia groaned. "Oh, Rex, don't do this to me. I've spent all day trying to separate what happened last night from the reality of today. I've been telling myself it was a one-time thing, and I'm lucky to have the memories. But it's very hard. Harder still if I get within touching distance. And cuddling under a blanket…"

"I know. I've had similar thoughts. I know we don't have the future, maybe not even tomorrow. But we do have right now. I can't imagine what you're going through, but you must need holding."

Rex was right. They were stuck in this van together, possibly for hours to come, and so long as they both knew the rules, what would it hurt to take small comfort from each other?

Tossing caution onto the floor and stomping on it, she scooted closer to him and he put his arm around her shoulders, tucking her snugly against him. They worked together to arrange the blanket around their shoulders and drape it across their laps, leaving them each one arm free to use binoculars.

"Did your grandmother ever say what caused her PTSD?" Rex asked a little too casually.

Nadia's breath caught in her throat. The fact that he'd reopened that line of conversation could only mean one thing—he was looking for a way to open up about his own experiences. Big, strong men often had more trouble dealing with post-traumatic stress disorder because they didn't like sharing their experiences aloud. They seemed to think it wasn't manly to open up and prided themselves on keeping everything inside and dealing with it alone.

"I'm not sure there was any one thing with Nana," she said. "Her life in Russia is something we pampered Americans have a hard time understanding. Even the poorest of our poor don't live like she did, alternately freezing and starving. When she was four, her own grandmother froze to death during the night while Nana slept next to her. The ground was frozen so hard they couldn't bury her, they had to just leave her out in the snow. She saw death, violent death and a lot of it, her whole life. It was why she was able to be trained to kill. She became…what's the word? Inured. Inured to the violence and death."

"Numb on the outside," Rex said in a way that let Nadia know he understood exactly. "But on some level she did feel it. Because she's human."

"The ones who cease to be human—those are the ones with real problems. They emerge from the killing fields and become mindless slaughter machines, disorganized serial killers."

"It sounds like you've done some studying."

"I thought at one time I might become a psychiatrist. I got my undergrad in psychology and even went to medical school for a year. But the hard sciences pulled me in. The physical world is a big enough mystery for me. The human mind, a little too scary."

"Mine certainly is."

"Your mind doesn't scare me. Nothing about you scares me."

Rex blew a breath out in a gusty sigh. It was cold enough now even inside the car that their breath was steaming. "Maybe it should."

"Why? Why do you say that?"

He hesitated, then plunged ahead. "You never saw me when I had my meltdown. I was a certifiable, gibbering idiot requiring a straitjacket."

It upset Nadia to picture that, but not for the reasons Rex thought. She didn't believe he was incompetent now, and she certainly didn't fear for her own safety around him, no matter what his past. She simply felt his pain. She knew it intimately. Nana had shared so much of her own guilt over the things she'd done, and they'd cried together. "This meltdown. Was there anything in particular that set it off?" He'd said it was a mission that went wrong but hadn't given any details.

Long, long silence. Nadia didn't push him. He would tell her when he was ready, or perhaps never. Finally, "My last assignment, I was ordered to kill a woman. A young, pregnant woman."

Now Nadia did react. She hadn't expected that. Intellectually she knew women could be as evil as men, that if they engaged in warfare and espionage they risked dying by the sword.

"We were in Korea, the Demilitarized Zone. There was a sniper who was picking off our men, and my job was to take him out." He took a deep, shaky breath and continued. "I didn't know my target was a woman until I was ready to pull the trigger. Then she turned, and I saw her belly—but by then it was too late to stop."

"So you killed her?"

He shook his head. "I learned later that she didn't die. But I did hit her. It was the first time I'd failed to make a kill—and the last time I ever tried. When I saw her fall, I dropped my gun, remembering the name and face of every person I'd killed, all piled on top of one another, and I thought about their loved ones left behind, wives and children, children they would never have, and…"

"You lost it."

"That's one way to put it. I'm lucky I had friends who were able to get me out of there, because I was in no condition to get out on my own. The Marines put me in Bethesda, gave me an honorable discharge. When I got out of the psych ward, I had a nice hunk of change waiting for me in a numbered Swiss bank account—a bribe to keep my mouth shut. And I have. Not even Lori or Ace know the details of what I did overseas. You're the only person I've ever told."

"Had you made a mistake? Or was this pregnant woman the sniper?"

"She was the sniper. I learned later that her husband had been killed by a very old land mine—probably dating from the Korean war. She held Americans responsible, and it was her life mission to kill as many as she could." He took another breath. "She killed at least six more after she recovered from the gunshot wound I gave her."

There was a long silence before Nadia finally asked, "Why me? Why would you trust me with this information?" She made a point of peering through her binoculars. Her hand trembled noticeably, but perhaps Rex would think she was shivering with the cold.

"Because I knew you would understand. And maybe because you have a right to know exactly the sort of man into whose hands you've put your daughter's life."

"Nothing you say will change my mind about that," Nadia said. "You're the one who can bring her home, if anyone can."

"What if I can't shoot?"

"If the need arises, you will do what has to be done. I have complete faith in you."

"I can't imagine why."

She shrugged. She didn't know why she was so sure of him, his motives, his character, his very essence. But she was. Though he took great pains to hide his true self behind the rough, tough man of action, she'd been able to see into his soul almost from the hour they'd met.

"I appreciate your confiding in me," she said. "Especially when I've been less than a hundred percent forthcoming myself."

"I understand security regulations."

Yes, and he'd just violated several by telling her of his work in Korea. Obviously he trusted her completely. "I'm working in nanotechnology at JanCo Labs."

"I sort of figured that out. You said something to Peter about a nano. Nadia, you don't have to tell me. Unless it's information I need to do this job better—"

"You're risking your life for my daughter. If you're going to kill, or be killed, you have a right to know the stakes involved. It's life or death, but not just one life or hundreds or thousands. It's the future of the entire planet."

REX HAD NO IDEA how to reply to that. If that statement about the end of the world had come from anyone else, he would instantly conclude they were crazy. But Nadia was one of the most sane, down-to-earth people he'd ever met, not the type to inflate her importance with wild stories.

Finally he settled on a response. "You aren't going to leave me hanging there, are you?"

"Do you know much about nanotechnology?"

"Small stuff, right? Constructing chemicals and machines at the molecular level." He'd read some about nanomachines. Information had filtered beyond scientific journals and into the popular culture, and he liked to keep up with science and technology. She turned around to look at him, maybe to see whether he was kidding or not. "Hey, I got a brain."

She smiled. "I know that."

"So you're working on making little machines?"

"Specifically, tiny assemblers that convert organic waste into something resembling crude oil."

"Wow. I thought stuff like that was decades into the future."

"So did we. It was a surprise breakthrough, an accident, really, a couple of years ago."

"Your breakthrough?"

"Me and a couple of colleagues. Needless to say, we got unlimited funds from the U.S. government to work on it. The technology has the potential to solve the world's energy problems."

"I take it there's a catch."

"A rather large one. You need a lot of assemblers—millions and millions—to create even a small amount of fuel oil. It would take eons to build them, so they have to be self-replicating. And once they start replicating…"

"Like rabbits?"

She nodded. "Given enough raw material, in just ten hours an unchecked self-replicating autoassembler would spawn sixty-eight billion offspring, all starving for more raw material."

"And the raw material is…"

"Anything organic. Garbage, plants, animals and people. In less than two days the autoassemblers would outweigh the Earth."

"My God, you're talking about gray goo, aren't you." A shiver slithered up Rex's spine. Some scientists had been preaching caution when it came to nanotechnology because they believed an out-of-control nanomachine could reduce the earth to nothing but glop. But they were a small minority. "I thought gray goo was a myth."

"It may be. We don't really know what would happen if the stuff went unchecked. But a very real possibility exists that the entire earth could become nothing but a rock coated with petroleum sludge."

"Which makes your little lab experiment potentially one of the most lethal weapons ever known, right up there with the atomic bomb."

"Bingo. Peter says he wants it so America won't have a monopoly on such a powerful technology, that every country has the right to cheap energy. But who's to say that once he has it in his hands, he won't sell it to the highest bidder, whether that was Russia or Iran or whoever?"

"My God," Rex said again.

"Before we were divorced, Peter asked me to smuggle a sample of the Petro-Nano—that's what we call it—from the lab. I put together a fake, to placate him. I thought he would go back to Russia and I could report him. But he figured out I'd double-crossed him. That was when—" Her voice broke. "That was when he broke my jaw. But he must be crazy to think I would put something so dangerous in any civilian's hands."

"Not even to save Lily's life?"

"Only to have her turned into sludge with every other human? No. I love my daughter, and I would give up my life for her in a heartbeat. But others' lives are not mine to bargain with."

Rex knew in that instant he felt more than simple lust for Nadia. The realization shocked him. He'd always thought "falling in love" was a silly notion, a romantic rationalization humans had come up with to justify a perfectly natural biological urge to mate that, in his mind, didn't need justification.

But there it was; his heart had just inflated to three sizes beyond normal and the back of his throat ached with the swell of emotion he felt for this incredibly strong, compassionate, intelligent woman who trusted him enough to violate national security regulations— and put her daughter's life in his hands.

She hadn't yet labeled him a nutcase despite all the evidence he'd given her, but if she knew what he was thinking now, she probably would call for the men in the white coats.

"Look, there," Nadia said suddenly. Her body tensed and she sat up straighter, letting the blanket fall off her shoulder. "That old car, pulling into the driveway of that white house. Isn't that the car Peter was driving at the mall?"

"That car was stolen. He abandoned it later that day. But this is the same model, a couple of years newer. He might have stolen another one. Car thieves tend to have their preferences and stick with them."

"Is it worth a closer look?"

"Definitely."

The car, which was blue rather than green, had pulled into the one-car garage behind one of Nadia's target houses. A man in a raincoat emerged from the garage, pulled the door down, then headed for a back door.

"Is it him?" Rex asked.

"I can't tell, with the hood of his coat pulled around his face like that. But he's the right size and shape."

"And he's coming home at an odd hour. It's only a little after four. Most of the people in this neighborhood will be getting home after five, when the factories have their shift changes."

"What should we do?"

"Get a closer look. You keep watching. I'm going to see what all Lori has back here in her van-o-tricks."

Rex was too big to squeeze through the gap made by the armrest as Nadia had, so he opened his door, climbed out and quickly ran around to the back and entered through the double doors without getting too wet. He rummaged around in various storage compartments until he found what he needed—a utility repairman's coveralls, complete with legitimate logo. Another boyfriend of Lori's had provided them. A hard hat would lend authority to the costume. There was even a bogus ID badge.

Rex decided to cross the street on foot carrying a toolbox, go to the door and use some story about needing to get into the backyard to check something.

Via his headset, he let the others know his plan. "Beau, you drive up the alley and park just out of view in case anyone tries to escape out the back. Craig, after I ring the bell, pull into the driveway of the house next door. I'll tuck my headset just inside my collar and leave the channel open. If I give the word, prepare to move in."

"What about me?" Lori asked, having obviously grabbed Craig's headset from him, since Rex hadn't given her one.

He could hardly leave her out of it. "You're Craig's backup." As he talked, Rex took off his leather jacket and stepped into the coveralls, wishing he had some work boots to go with the costume. His running shoes would look conspicuous. But hopefully whoever answered the door wouldn't be looking down at his shoes.

"What do you want me to do?" Nadia asked.

"You'll stay here with your cell phone and dial 9-1-1 if things go south."

"I could help," she argued. "I could hide in the bushes and maybe dart in and take Lily to safety—"

"No. Nadia, you're not trained in this type of work."

"I certainly know how to grab a baby and run."

"No," he repeated. "I can't do my job if I'm having to worry about you." He almost told her right then that he was falling in love with her and couldn't bear for anything to happen to her. But he bit his lip just in time. She was so right when she pointed out there was no future for them. It would only make things harder on both of them if he admitted he felt more than physical attraction for her.

"I'm rolling," he said into the radio. "Is everyone else ready?"

He got affirmatives from everybody. But before exiting the van, he pushed the armrest forward and leaned through the gap, kissing a surprised Nadia. The kiss was hard and, by necessity, fast.

"Oh," was all she said.

"For luck. And courage." And because if anything did happen to him, he wanted Nadia's kiss to be one of his last memories. But he tried not to think too hard about his own mortality.

Toolbox in hand, he walked up the street to the crosswalk, across Dupree, then switched directions, heading for the white house. He saw Craig's car move into position, ready to turn into the driveway of the house next door.

"I'm in position," Beau said over the walkie-talkie.

"I'm almost there," Rex replied. "I'm taking off the

headset now, so I won't be able to hear you, but I'll leave the channel open so you can hear me. Beau, give me two sharp horn blasts if anything happens in your direction." He pulled off the headset and tucked it beneath the collar of his coveralls. Then he walked up to the porch and rang the doorbell.

He heard a baby crying inside, and his adrenaline surged.

A woman answered—young, thickset, definitely not the rat-faced woman of Nadia's description. She had a toddler on her hip, a blond-haired little girl. Rex's heart hammered inside his chest, but a half second later he realized the little girl was not Lily. No way.

"Hi, I'm from Payton Power & Light," he said with a friendly smile. "We've got some power outages in this area. You folks having any trouble?"

"No," the woman said, friendly as can be. "But we've had some trouble in the past, about six months ago. There was a big tree—you folks cut back the limbs, but maybe they grew out again."

"I just wanted to warn you I'll be in your backyard. The trouble's with some new residents—we went to turn the power on and it's not working."

"Maybe we're getting some ice buildup," the woman said, peering past Rex at the leaden sky. "You must mean those folks who moved in a couple of doors down."

"Yeah. A foreign couple, Russian I think," Rex said, grabbing the opportunity the woman had given him. "They got a cute little tyke about the same age as yours."

The woman frowned. "Oh, no, I was talking about an older couple, the Copelands. From Iowa."

"Honey, who is it?" A man's voice. The man himself soon appeared, still wearing his wet raincoat. Not Peter.

"It's a man from PP&L," the woman said. "He says we have more new neighbors, a Russian couple with a baby Kayla's age. We'll have to keep an eye out for them."

"I guess there's a lot of people moving into the neighborhood," Rex said, adding a folksy laugh. "Thanks for your trouble."

"No problem." She shut the door, and Rex let out a long breath as he grabbed the headset and put it back on.

"Did you copy that?" he asked the others. "False alarm."

The others acknowledged they'd heard.

Rex was still cursing their damnable luck as he trudged back toward the crosswalk when a hand reached out from a bush and snagged his arm. He yelped in surprise, his fight-or-flight instincts in full flower, ready to deck whoever had invaded his space—until he realized it was Nadia.

"What are you doing here?" he demanded. "You were supposed to stay in the car."

"I saw that the woman had a baby. It looked like Lily. I couldn't stay all the way across the street."

"It wasn't Lily." He dragged her out of the shrubs where she'd been hiding. She was thoroughly wet and bedraggled looking, and so beguiling he didn't know whether to shake her or kiss her.

He did neither, of course.

"I wasn't going to interfere," she began again. "But I needed to see what was going on—"

"We've had this discussion before," he said curtly,

dragging her along with him as he neared the corner. He didn't want to miss the light. He'd had enough of standing in the rain. "When I give an order, I expect it to be followed."

"I just lose my good sense when it comes to Lily, I guess," she said miserably.

He knew it was true. The only other time she hadn't done exactly as he'd told her was at the mall, when she thought Peter would take her to Lily. The light refused to turn green, so he just crossed the street against it, earning a couple of honks.

As they reached the other side of Dupree, Nadia pulled her arm out of his grasp. "Look, for the record, I don't like being dragged around like a sack of potatoes. I don't like being pushed around at all. I've put my life—everything that's important to me—in your total control because I had no other choice. But I'm not stupid, and I wouldn't have done anything to interfere with your actions. Maybe I was putting myself at a slight risk, but that's my choice to make."

"Then I will leave you at home next time."

"Hey, who's paying for this operation?"

"I haven't seen the money yet."

Nadia knew she had to get away from Rex before she said or did something she would regret. There was a gas station on the next corner. She desperately needed a bathroom and a hot cup of coffee. "I'll be back in five minutes."

"You can't just—"

"I can. Please, just for once do what someone else asks. Go back to the van, watch those houses—Peter could have come and gone ten times while we were standing here arguing. I'll get us coffee from that gas station. Maybe by the time I return, we'll both have cooled down."

Rex started to argue some more, but in the end he let her go.

THE FREEZING RAIN fell in earnest now, tiny balls of ice that stung when they hit Nadia's skin. She hurried across 42nd Street to the gas station and mini-mart. Inside it was warm and dry, and she just stood there a moment absorbing the heat.

The store was slightly shabby, with narrow aisles stuffed to the gills with junk food and a seating area with two tables, neither of which had been wiped down recently.

Normally chips and cookies didn't tempt her, but she was starving. But first things first. She got the key to the women's bathroom from the teenage clerk. Thankfully, the bathroom was inside, though it wasn't much bigger than a shower stall. She took care of business, washed her hands, then emerged to peruse the racks of fat- and pre-servative-laden goodies, wondering what Rex would like.

She shouldn't have lost her temper, she knew. He'd been right. She should have followed his orders because he knew best. But the frustration, the powerlessness, had gotten to her—to both of them, apparently. To believe they almost had Peter, then feel the crushing disappointment when they realized the man was not Peter, the baby not Lily—it was almost too much to bear. So she would bring a peace offering and apologize.

Let's see, was Rex a Cheez Doodles man? Definitely not. She was leaning toward beef jerky—the extra-hot kind—when the bell above the store's door jingled. She didn't look up until the newcomer spoke to the clerk.

"Do you have milk?" A soft voice. Faintly accented. Peter's voice?

Her heart slammed against her ribs. What were the chances? He was hiding out in this neighborhood, but why here, why now when she was without resources, without backup?

She was in the center aisle. She chanced a peek around the corner and verified that it was, indeed, her ex-husband, looking very normal in work pants, a denim shirt and an old nylon parka. She ducked out of sight.

Peter started down the next aisle over, near the refrigerator cases. Nadia pulled the hood of her sweatshirt over her hair and kept her back to him, pretending to study the candy bars. Her breath came in short, harsh gasps, echoing in her ears. It sounded so loud she was sure Peter would be able to hear her.

He wouldn't notice her. She was the only other person in the store, but how often did people really notice other customers when they were shopping?

She heard a refrigerator case open, then close. Peter's rubber-soled shoes lightly thumped their way toward the cashier. She just had to stand here unobtrusively a few more seconds and it would all be over. Then she could watch as he left, see where he went, run back to the van.

She was so close to Lily now, she could almost feel the baby in her arms. Maybe Lily was in Peter's car. She stood on tiptoe and tried to peer over the food shelves, but she was too short.

"One minute," Peter said. "Diapers."

"In the very back," the clerk said in a bored voice, completely oblivious to the relationship between his two customers.

This time Peter headed straight down the center aisle—straight for her. She kept her gaze resolutely toward the snacks. He brushed past her with a murmured "Excuse me." She almost let herself breathe.

Then his footsteps slowed, and stopped. There was a squeak of rubber sole as he pivoted around. She dared a peek sideways at him, and he was staring at her with malevolent green eyes.

Could she possibly pretend this was a coincidence? But she could tell from the expression on his face that he already knew it wasn't. Before she could do anything—scream, fight, run—he grabbed her and held her in a headlock. She flailed harmlessly, succeeding only in dashing a row of chips to the floor.

"Don't make any noise," he growled into her ear. "I've got a gun pointed at your head."

"Hey!" The clerk had apparently noticed the struggle.

Peter's reaction was immediate and violent. He extended his arm, and he was indeed holding a gun, a huge Smith & Wesson .45.

"Hands up, and do not even think about hitting an alarm button. We are leaving, and if you are smart you will live to tell your children about this."

The clerk thrust his arms skyward, utterly terrified.

While Peter's attention was on the clerk, Nadia continued to struggle, but she stilled when he brought the gun back to her head. "Be still."

"You won't kill me," Nadia said, praying that by some miracle, Rex was paying attention, had been watching her. He was protective of her. But his priority would be the job, so his attention was more likely to be on the houses he was supposed to be watching. "You need me."

"I'll kill you if that's what it takes to survive. But then what will happen to poor Lily? Orphan girls don't fare well in Russia."

Nadia immediately ceased struggling. She couldn't bear to think of Lily neglected in some orphanage. "All right, I'll go with you," she said softly.

Peter shifted his grip to an armlock, guiding her along almost effortlessly. The slightest hesitation on her part brought excruciating pain to her shoulder and elbow, and she knew he could break it with only a small effort. The clerk followed their departure with terrified eyes, and she felt a moment of pity for him, for the helplessness he must be feeling.

At the last moment, Peter fired his gun. The large mirror behind the clerk shattered and the clerk fell, or ducked, Nadia wasn't sure which. She hoped he hadn't been hit. It would be on her head if anything happened to that poor boy.

Peter dragged her to his vehicle, a beat-up white minivan. He opened the back door, obviously intending to toss her inside. Self-preservation instincts kicked in and Nadia renewed her struggles, hoping to somehow break free. But Peter hit her in the head with the gun, and blackness engulfed her.

Chapter Eleven

Rex knew he'd been a jerk. But he'd thought for sure they were about to break the case and bring Lily home. The signs had looked good. Maybe he'd been too optimistic, too anxious to be Nadia's hero. Maybe he hadn't read the signs with realistic expectations.

After his failure, his frustrations had bubbled to the surface, and he'd taken it out on Nadia, who truthfully hadn't done anything to jeopardize the operation. She'd been two houses away, and so well concealed he'd almost walked right by her. Although he still believed team members should follow orders, he had to give her high marks for chutzpah.

If this was the way he treated a woman he thought he was falling in love with, how badly had he treated the others? No wonder they didn't stick around. Maybe he needed more therapy, much as he resisted. Was there a special therapy for a sexist bastard with a bad attitude? A twelve-step program?

He'd just settled in to resume his watch on the target houses when he heard the shot.

There was no mistaking it. It wasn't a car backfire or

a firecracker. It was a gun, and the report had come from the direction of the gas station where Nadia had gone.

He started up the van and careened onto Dupree toward the gas station. "Gunfire at the Conoco station, Dupree and 42nd. I'm checking it out. Nadia's in there. Over."

"On my way," said Craig. "I heard it, too. Wait, it's coming over the police radio now. A holdup—no, a kidnapping!"

Nadia! Rex's stomach sank even as his adrenaline surged high enough to give him a heart attack. As he pulled into traffic, he saw a white minivan speed out of the gas station parking lot at an alarming speed, tires screeching.

"I'm in pursuit of a white Dodge minivan," he shouted into the walkie-talkie. "Texas plates, I'm not close enough to see the number. Heading east on 42nd Street." He gunned the van, and though Lori had made a few modifications to the beast to give it more get-up-and-go, it was not built for speed, especially going uphill, and the minivan was already putting distance between them.

Once it crested the hill, the Peepmobile picked up speed again. The minivan had slowed. Perhaps Peter was trying not to call attention to himself. If he could blend into traffic now, and no one got his plate numbers, he could get away. Rex dropped back farther, not wanting to spook him. Peter might not know he'd been followed.

If it was Peter. If this was even the right vehicle. Maybe the driver was simply an innocent bystander who'd heard shooting and gotten the hell out of there.

"Craig, I need info," Rex said into the headset radio, which had only a short range. "I'm almost out of range. Let's move to the CB."

They were back in touch moments later. "I've still got the white minivan in view," Rex said. "I need to know if I have the right vehicle." Craig, being on the police force, would be the best bet for getting accurate information in this situation.

"Stay on that van," Craig shot back. "According to the clerk, it was a man with a Russian accent, and he kidnapped a pretty girl with black hair and a hooded sweatshirt. He threw her into a white minivan."

"I'm tailing him, and I'm not sure he knows I'm here. I could use some backup." He provided the intersection he'd just passed.

"We're on our way," said Lori, who had apparently taken over communications.

"Me, too," Beau chimed in. "We'll tag team him."

It was an exercise Beau and Rex had practiced often enough, taking turns tailing a suspect so he wouldn't spot any one car too often.

Unfortunately, Peter noticed Rex behind him before they could put their tailing plan into action. Rex knew the minute he'd been spotted. The minivan suddenly accelerated, then made a series of dazzling twists and turns, moving with surprising speed and agility.

There was no way Rex could keep up for long, and the minivan was getting farther and farther ahead of him.

"I'm dying here, I need help." Beau's souped-up Mustang would come in handy for this kind of chase.

Rex related street names as they passed by in a blur, and after what seemed like an eternity he saw the black muscle car behind him.

Moments later it screeched past him.

"He turned left about six blocks up!" Rex yelled into the radio. Another few seconds, and the Mustang turned, also. By the time Rex made the turn, both cars were out of sight. "Do you have him?"

Beau's answer was a series of curses that would have embarrassed a longshoreman. "He had too big a lead on me. I never even saw him."

They roamed the neighborhood independently for a few minutes, hoping to get lucky and stumble upon the van, but Rex knew with sick certainty that it was a lost cause. Peter had gotten away.

Nadia was gone.

Damn, he should have anticipated that risk. He shouldn't have allowed Nadia to let herself be so visible right in Peter's backyard. Granted, it had involved supreme bad luck that Peter had picked that moment to buy gas at his neighborhood station, but any operative worth his salt *counted* on supreme bad luck.

His only consolation was that Peter wouldn't kill Nadia, not so long as he believed there was any chance Nadia would give him what he wanted. She had sworn to Rex she wouldn't cave in to Peter's demands, under any circumstances. But now that she was under her ex-husband's control, all bets were off. If he was connected to the Russian Mafia, which was a definite possibility, he was in the company of people who knew how to make reluctant hostages cooperate.

Rex didn't even want to consider what means they might use.

"We'll never find him this way," Beau said.

"Let's meet at the office," Rex returned wearily. "Plan our next move."

"What about the houses on Dupree?" Beau asked. "Peter probably won't be dumb enough to return, knowing how close Nadia was to his hideout. But what if her baby and the rat-faced woman are still there?"

Damn. Rex had been so focused on Nadia's fate, he'd almost forgotten about Lily. They might still be able to recover Nadia's baby. Then they would only need to focus on one hostage.

But Craig's next words dashed his hopes. "Witnesses reported seeing a woman with a baby in the van. They're all together."

And they had all slipped through the net.

ACE WAS ON HIS WAY HOME from the airport when the kidnapping occurred, and Gavin was in his car on his way back from Dallas. The two men joined the war party at the First Strike office. Rex had a full complement of experienced bounty hunters at his disposal, a seasoned detective in Craig, plus Lori and her estimable computer hacking skills.

In addition, the Payton Police Department had opened an official investigation into what they were calling a foiled robbery and subsequent kidnapping. While Craig drove back to First Strike, he'd been on the phone trying to find out what all the police knew.

"At this point, their information is thin," Craig reported to the group. "They have sketchy descriptions of the van, the suspect and the victim."

"Any video surveillance?" Rex asked.

Craig shook his head. "The store had a video camera, but it was incorrectly aimed, so all they got were pictures of the clerk."

Ace shook his head. "Idiots."

"So the question is, do we tell them what we know?" Beau asked. "Give them names, descriptions, motives? The police could get the information out to the media."

They all looked at Rex, putting the decision on him.

"Who's in charge of the kidnapping case?" he asked Craig.

"You're not going to like it."

Everyone in the room groaned. "Not Lyle Palmer," Rex said, voicing everyone's worst fears.

"'Fraid so."

Lori made an exasperated sound. "Who is that guy sleeping with to get assigned every high-profile crime to hit Payton?"

Rex envisioned going to Lyle and telling him the whole story. He would have to hold back the part about the Petro-Nano, of course. Nadia had trusted him with that information, and nothing in the world would make him betray that trust. But Lyle would want to know the motive for the kidnapping.

Rex could pass it off as a domestic crime, a spurned ex-husband trying to get his wife and kid back. That might work.

"He'll screw it up," Gavin said, as if he could read Rex's thoughts. "Bet on it."

"I haven't exactly done stellar work the last day and a half," Rex said.

"Maybe we should go higher up," Lori suggested. "Homeland Security."

"It would take forever to work our way through Homeland Security to get to someone who could actually do something," Rex said. "We might not have that long. Originally Peter specified midnight tomorrow as his deadline. But now that he has Nadia…" He let his voice trail off.

"Is Peter looking for information?" Ace asked Rex. "Or a physical thing?"

"It's a physical thing," Rex answered. "Which means she has to go to JanCo to get it. And even if she only pretends to comply with Peter's demands, she might well go there to buy herself some time."

"I know the security director at JanCo," Ace said, which was typical. Ace knew everybody—he had an incredible database of contacts ranging from foreign dictators to the guy who sold newspapers downtown. He remembered their names and their kids' names, probably their pets, too. "We could bring him in."

"If we're planning to launch any kind of operation at JanCo, we *have* to bring him in," Beau said. And again, they looked at Rex.

He nodded. Rex was relieved that the others hadn't urged him to turn this case over to the Payton cops or government agencies. On one hand, it would be a relief for someone else to take over responsibility for saving Nadia and Lily. On the other hand, he knew everyone on this team, knew they were some of the most intelligent, capable operatives he'd ever worked with. Even Gavin, who was Beau's brother-in-law and had been hired right out of prison to do skip-tracing, had quickly proved himself indispensable and was now a full member of the team.

Given the kind of small-scale operation they were contemplating, he would pit his team against anybody, anywhere. They had the experience, the equipment and firsthand knowledge of Peter and Nadia.

"I'll make the call," Ace said.

NADIA WAS FIRST AWARE of a dull, throbbing ache in her head and the taste of blood in her mouth. She'd bitten her tongue, she realized, gently running the injury along her teeth to see how bad it was.

Gradually, as full consciousness returned, she discovered she was tied up, her hands behind her, and she was in a moving vehicle. She knew she should be frightened out of her wits, but she was so consumed with trying to remember how she'd gotten here that her fears were merely nibbling at the edge of consciousness.

Then she remembered in a rush—Peter. He'd spotted her at the mini-mart. She didn't remember exactly what had happened, but clearly she'd been knocked out, so a slight memory loss would be normal. Nana had been hit in the head once and had lost an entire week. Nadia supposed she was lucky she'd only lost a few minutes. At least, she thought that was all.

Now, to the present. Peter had kidnapped her. Had Rex seen? Or had he been focused on the 4200 block of Dupree Street, oblivious to events occurring just up the block? By the time he missed her, she could be miles away.

She had a blanket over her, but since she'd been trussed up like a rodeo calf she couldn't toss it off, couldn't move at all. Maybe it would be best if she feigned unconsciousness, if she made Peter believe he'd injured her more severely than was the case.

She listened. A car radio played a news station. The car rolled along smoothly, not stopping for lights, so they weren't in city traffic. Where was he taking her? Would she be hauled out to the countryside and executed? If Peter had determined she'd double-crossed him, he might not be satisfied with merely killing her. And what about Lily?

As she lay there, despair washed over her. But at least she knew one thing: Lily was still alive, and she was being cared for. Why else would Peter have been buying milk and diapers?

She heard a noise, and her ears strained to identify it. Was it—could it be?—then she heard it again.

Lily! Her baby was in the car with her, only a few feet away, and she was fretting. It was all Nadia could do not to cry out to her child.

"Oh, God, would you just shut up?" an annoyed female voice said. It was the rat-faced woman, Peter's girlfriend. "I swear, all this kid does is eat, pee and cry."

Peter laughed. "That's what all babies do, Denise."

"No wonder I never want kids."

"You don't strike me as the maternal kind," he agreed.

"So what are we going to do with her?" Denise

asked, and Nadia knew she was no longer talking about Lily. "What if you killed her?"

"I didn't hit her hard enough to kill her. She'll come around."

"Then what?"

"Then we do what we should have done in the first place. We make her bring us a sample of the stuff."

"She hasn't done it yet. She was trying to double-cross you. We already know she has help."

"If that one guy in the beat-up van is the best she can do, we have nothing to worry about."

A guy in a beat-up van could only be Rex. That was encouraging—at least he knew what had happened to her. He'd seen the car Peter was driving. If there was ever a time to bring in the police, this would be it. If Peter got pulled over now, the game would be up.

But clearly no one was chasing them now. And Peter would no doubt ditch this vehicle at the first opportunity.

Her theory proved itself out a few minutes later. The car they were in pulled to a stop, and Peter cut the engine. Without saying much, they got out, opened a back door, and together wrestled Nadia out. She did her best to go completely limp. Nana Tania had once told her that the key to pretending you were asleep was to slacken your eyes and your jaw. She ordered every muscle to soften, and she slowed her breathing.

"Is she alive?" Denise asked fearfully.

"Yes, she's alive," Peter said impatiently. "I've got her. You get to work wiping down the van."

Nadia was dumped in the trunk of another car. But she'd gotten a glimpse of both vehicles when the wind had whipped her blanket aside briefly. Not that she thought the knowledge would help much, but she'd just been put into the trunk of a gold Lincoln Town Car, an older model.

Nadia had also seen where they were parked, but that wasn't any use. They were in a rural area, a field. She'd seen no identifying landmarks.

The Lincoln's trunk backed right up against the back seats, so Nadia could hear some of the conversation going on up front once they took off again.

"Can't we go back to Vlad's house?" Denise asked in a whining voice. "I'm tired of staying in dumps."

"Vlad would kill us if we brought hostages to his place. That's what we have safe houses for."

Vlad. Confirmation of what Rex and the other bounty hunters had already figured out—Peter's cigar-smoking gun-club friend was very much involved in this.

Peter and Denise were stupid to talk so freely in front of her, even if they did think she was unconscious. Stupid—or they didn't expect her to live to tell anyone anything.

Though Nadia had trouble judging the time—every minute stretched out to excruciating proportions when one was tied up in a car trunk—it seemed to be about twenty minutes later that the Lincoln reentered city traffic. She could see the lights of other cars flashing through cracks, and the car stopped at several intersections and made a few turns. Eventually it pulled to a stop. Again she was hauled out of the trunk. Peter threw her over his shoulder in a fireman's carry. She was able to see the house—a cheap, tract ranch house on a street of identical houses.

If she were able to get hold of a phone and call for help, she would not be able to identify where she was. But the chances of that were slim anyway. She'd left her cell phone in the Peepmobile.

Peter threw her onto a lumpy sofa. She cracked her eye just enough to see she was in a generic living room with white walls and beige carpet. So this was what a Russian Mafia safe house looked like.

He yanked the blanket all the way off her. "Nadia, wake up."

She lay as still as death.

"Maybe this will help." Denise's voice. A few moments later, a glass of water was dumped over Nadia's face. But she'd suspected something like that was coming and she managed to show no reaction.

Peter hauled her to a semiupright seated position. Nadia let her head loll to one side. Peter patted her cheeks. "C'mon, Nadia, rise and shine. Nadia?"

The vicious, blistering slap came out of nowhere, and this time Nadia wasn't able to hide her reaction. She jerked in shock and her eyes flew open. Her cheek stung as if it were burned, and her concussed head went from dull ache to crushing pain, all in the space of a half second.

Peter smiled cruelly. "I thought that might perk you up."

Nadia looked up at him. She wanted him to see hatred and defiance, but what she felt at that moment was raw fear. She'd managed to suppress the memories of the physical pain Peter had inflicted on her, but now they came flooding back. An open-palm slap was the least of her worries.

"If you want my cooperation," she said, her voice sounding a bit thick, "you won't touch me again."

Peter laughed. "And, as I've said before, you are in no position to make demands. You'll cooperate, all right. And you'll start off by telling me what you were doing at that gas station."

"Buying coffee."

He slapped her again.

"I was in the neighborhood visiting a friend," she said, trying desperately not to cry.

"You always go on social calls when your baby is missing?"

"She's Russian. I suspected you were working for the Russians, and I was hoping she might have heard something. I certainly never expected to run into you!"

"And who is this friend?"

"Glenda Bokolov," she said. "She lives on 42nd Street." Glenda was a real person, an old friend of her grandmother's. She had ties to the intelligence community, and Peter might recognize her name as legitimate. But he would never find her, so would not be able to discredit the story.

Peter considered the false information. Clearly he wasn't taking it at face value, but he didn't disbelieve it outright, either. "You and your bounty hunter friend. He was with you, no?"

"Yes."

"He gave chase. I killed him."

"I don't believe you!" she said quickly. Rex, killed? Oh, God, no. It couldn't be. Inside, she felt herself crumbling in hopelessness. But she refused to show

Peter what she felt. She continued to stare back at him defiantly.

"He was driving an old van. I am sure his brains made a horrible mess of the interior."

Now she knew he was trying to get an emotional reaction out of her. She would not give him the satisfaction, no matter how horrifying the picture he painted.

"Your lover is dead," he tried again. "There is no one to save you now."

Still, she refused to react. He slapped her again, harder than last time. She couldn't help it—she sobbed, and it made Peter smile. He raised his hand again, and this time he made a fist. She cringed and braced herself for the blow, but found the presence of mind to say, "Peter, I can't walk into JanCo with bruises on my face. It would invite extra scrutiny I don't need if you expect me to get you the Petro-Nano."

To her immense relief, her logic stopped him. "So you're going to do it?"

"Of course. What choice do I have as long as you have Lily? But I want to see my baby to make sure she's all right. Won't you please let me see Lily, let me hold her?"

"*Your* baby. Not *ours?*"

"Of course she's ours." It was all Nadia could do not to let loose with what she was really thinking—that he was a paranoid, delusional monster and she would never in a million years put a potentially powerful weapon into his hands. But she had to maintain the illusion that she intended to cooperate.

He reached out and stroked her face where he'd struck her. She tried not to let her revulsion show.

"Ah, Nadia, we could have been good together. You had so much potential—intelligence, beauty and a high security clearance. We could have used your assets to level the world playing field, take some of the marbles away from America. And we could have gotten rich in the process. But unfortunately you have this ridiculous streak of patriotism for a greedy, paternalistic country that thinks it should rule the world." He spat on the floor. "You're Russian, for God's sake. Your grandmother was a legend in the KGB."

"I'm an American," she said wearily.

"Because your Russian mother had the bad sense to let an American impregnate her? He didn't stick around long, did he?"

"He died. And this country gave my grandmother sanctuary when her own people would have liquidated her, a fact you conveniently forget. Make no mistake, Peter. If you become inconvenient, your wonderful Russian friends will get rid of you without the slightest twinge of conscience."

His face twisted into a harsh mask. "You know nothing about my friends."

"I know they've lied to you about why they want the Petro-Nano. They say they want cheap energy available to all. What they really want is a weapon of mass destruction they can use to blackmail anyone they choose."

The smile he gave her chilled her to the bone. "I understand more than you think, darling."

Behind Peter, Nadia caught a glimpse of Denise peeking around a doorway at them, smoking furiously.

Her expression was one of frank jealousy. She'd probably overheard the entire conversation, and she did not like her boyfriend having such an intimate exchange with his ex-wife.

Nadia wondered how she could use Denise's jealousy for her own benefit.

Peter abruptly stood and hauled Nadia to her feet. He swiveled her around and cut the stocking he'd used to tie her wrists. "Enough talk. We'll go to JanCo now and you will get the Petro-Nano. After I have verified the sample is genuine, I will release you and Lily. But if you even think about betraying me, you will not see your daughter again."

"How will you verify it? There are only a handful of scientists in the world who understand this technology enough to know what they're looking at."

"I will be able to verify the contents," Peter said smugly. "If you try to fool me as you did before, you will get worse than a broken jaw."

Nadia didn't doubt it. She would lose her life this time.

"You need to clean up, make yourself presentable so that you may visit your place of employment without garnering suspicion."

"You want me to go tonight?"

"There is no reason to wait. The sooner we get this matter taken care of, the sooner you can get your daughter back and resume your life."

"What time is it?"

"Why?"

"I can't get into the lab after eight o'clock. They instituted new security measures. The building is locked down after 8:00 p.m., based on recommendations from Homeland Security." She prayed Peter wouldn't catch her in the lie. It sounded reasonable enough. Security measures were in a constant state of flux at JanCo, but at her clearance level she could come and go as she pleased.

Peter cursed. "We'll have to wait until tomorrow."

"I won't be able to get the sample during the day while other workers are around. The best time would be after five, when almost everyone is gone. I called in sick the last two days. I can do the same tomorrow, then come in late in the afternoon and say I'm feeling better and I want to catch up on a few things. No one will question me working late under those circumstances."

Nadia hated the thought of spending another day as Peter's prisoner. But the more time she gave to Rex and his team, the better chance they would have of foiling Peter's plans and getting her and Lily out alive.

Peter pursed his lips. "All right. Late tomorrow afternoon."

"May I see Lily now?" When his face hardened, she quickly added, "What difference will it make? I've told you I'll give you what you want. Letting me see Lily won't change anything."

"You can see your brat when I have what I want."

Peter allowed her to use the bathroom, wash her face, brush her teeth. She went through the motions numbly, trying not to think too hard about what Peter had said. Surely he hadn't really killed Rex. Peter had just been trying to break her down. But if it was true? *No, no, don't think, just brush. Up and down, up and down.*

She hoped that Peter would not restrain her again, that he would believe his threats about Lily would ensure she wouldn't try to escape. But when she emerged from the bathroom, he led her to one of the dining-room chairs, where he secured her with duct tape.

"I won't be able to sleep like this," she protested. "The work you're requiring of me tomorrow is exacting. I can't do it if I'm delirious from lack of sleep."

"You can sleep tomorrow. For tonight, I want you secure so that *I* can sleep."

"I don't see how you *can* sleep." She couldn't resist. "Doesn't your conscience gnaw at your insides like a rat?"

Without warning, he punched her in the stomach so hard she retched. "I can do many things to you that won't leave marks," he said as she writhed and gasped, trying to get some air back into her lungs. "Keep that in mind next time you're tempted to be smart."

Chapter Twelve

After sitting upright in a supremely uncomfortable position for the entire night, Nadia was allowed to lie down the next day when Peter could keep a close watch on her. She was given water but no food, then commanded to sleep.

She knew she had to sleep. Her mind was already sluggish from lack of food and rest, and she would need as much strength as she could muster if she wanted to get through the next few hours. Still, as she lay on the lumpy, musty sofa, she found herself struggling to stay awake in case Lily cried or called for her.

At some point her baby did cry from the other end of the house. Though it tore at Nadia's heart to hear those sounds of distress and be helpless to do anything about it, she was nonetheless reassured that Lily was alive. She was finally able to fall asleep.

Later, she was able to take a shower. When she emerged, she found some clean clothes and a few basic toiletries. Peter would know that she normally did not go to work in jeans, so he'd provided her with a casual pair of slacks and a sweater, even some under-things.

How very thoughtful, she fumed as she put on the discount-store clothes. They fit well, and though they weren't high quality, they were in a style she might have bought herself. Peter knew her tastes and it irritated her.

When she came out, he handed her a cheese sandwich. "Eat that," he ordered. "I don't want you passing out before you've served your purpose."

She ate the sandwich, thinking it tasted wonderful. She hadn't eaten in nearly twenty-four hours. She was given a canned soft drink, too. The sleep and the boost to her blood sugar cleared her head, allowed her to think rationally again.

And with rational thought came a radical idea. She'd been racking her brain trying to come up with some way out of this situation, some way to save her life and Lily's without giving Peter what he wanted. And her ideas had done nothing but chase their tails. She'd been given a Hobson's Choice—her daughter's life, or potentially the lives of millions, billions of people.

That was no choice at all.

To Nadia's surprise, just as she finished her scant meal Denise strolled into the dining room with Lily slung casually on her hip, as if they hadn't spent the last umpteen hours deliberately keeping mother and daughter separated. Lily took one look at Nadia, gave a shriek of joy and held out her arms to Nadia. Instinctively Nadia was out of her chair and lunging for her daughter, but Peter grabbed her by the arm and held her in check.

Was he so cruel that he would bring them this close and not let them touch?

But then he relented. "Let her hold the brat," he said carelessly.

"Gladly," Denise said, practically tossing the baby at Nadia.

Nadia gathered Lily into her arms and squeezed her hard. She was dirty and smelly and probably hadn't had her diaper changed in some time, given that Peter hadn't been able to complete his Pampers purchase last night. But she was the most wonderful little lump of humanity Nadia had ever felt. She buried her nose in Lily's silky brown hair and inhaled deeply. Ah, yes, baby shampoo, still discernible.

"Lily, oh Lily, my precious one."

Lily, overwhelmed, started crying.

"Oh, no, darling, don't cry. Mama's here."

"That's charming," Denise said sourly. "Is she always so happy to see Mommy?"

Nadia ignored Denise and focused on her baby. She did not know what the evening might bring, and this might be the very last time she saw her child. She struggled to commit the feeling of her to memory, to engrave it into her brain so that she would never, ever forget, in this world or the next.

"Please," she whispered into Lily's ear. "Remember me, too." But she knew Lily was too young to remember anything from this experience when she was older. Maybe that was a good thing.

A foreign noise, a metallic snapping, pulled Nadia from the bittersweet haze of her reunion with Lily. She focused on her ex-husband, and saw that he was holding a large pair of nippers. That alone should have frightened her, but the expression on his face was what she found truly terrifying. She'd never seen such naked cruelty.

"What are you doing?" she demanded.

"This tool is very sharp, very powerful. With it, I can lop off a half-inch tree branch with no problem. A baby's fingers will be easy work."

Nadia's every fiber froze with horror. "Oh, God. Peter, how could you possibly even think something like that? What evil's inside you—she's your own flesh and blood!"

"I very much doubt that. At any rate, I won't be doing the lopping. It will be Denise. And trust me, after taking care of your brat for two days, there is no love lost between Denise and Lily."

Nadia held on to Lily more tightly and focused on Denise. "You're a woman. How can you condone this hideousness? Do you have children?"

Denise sneered. "I grew up close to Chernobyl. I will never have children, thank God. I do not like them."

"And do you like being Peter's minion? Does he tell you he loves you? Don't you think he might be using you, too, just as he's now using me? Did he ever offer to change Lily's diaper, or did he make you do all the dirty work?"

Denise's expression faltered for a split second, and Nadia knew she'd made her point.

Peter knew, too. Abruptly he grabbed onto Lily and ripped her out of Nadia's grasp, then passed her off to Denise as if the baby might give him some disease. "That's enough. Denise will be following behind us in a separate car with Lily—and the tool. If you deviate from our plan in the slightest degree, she will know, and she will not hesitate to cause your daughter pain. If you betray me, Lily's death will not be fast or compassionate. She will die screaming in hideous pain. Is that very, very clear, darling?"

Nadia felt the blood drain from her head, and she swayed slightly on her feet. He was only trying to scare her. He wouldn't do that. Denise wouldn't do that. But seeing the sick, self-satisfied expression on Denise's face, Nadia realized the woman could be cruel indeed. And she despised Nadia for having had Peter before her.

"It's very clear," Nadia said.

She and Peter climbed into the gold Town Car. He did not bother to tie her up. He knew his latest threat was incentive enough to keep her from attacking him or calling for help.

"Once we get to JanCo," Peter said, "we will park in the employee lot and you will go inside alone. I will stay in the car. Denise will be some distance away, watching from her car."

Nadia's mind raced. If she was allowed to go into JanCo alone—and with the company's security measures, there was no way Peter could get in with her— she had a chance. There were phones inside JanCo, people she could go to for help.

Peter laughed, jolting her. "I know what you're thinking. You will not be able to signal for help. You will be wearing a microphone, and I will be able to hear every word you say, every move you make. If you do anything we haven't agreed on…" He made a cutting motion with his fingers, grinning maniacally all the time.

He was actually enjoying this. He had no chance of succeeding with his plan. She would not give him the Petro-Nano. He would be arrested and spend the rest of his life incarcerated. But would Lily survive?

Nadia swallowed back tears of despair. How could she offer up the life of her own child? How could any mother? She would so much rather die herself than lose Lily.

The idea she'd only flirted with earlier jumped back into her mind. It was horrible. But it might be her only chance, her only choice—to not make a choice.

Yes, that was the answer. As they drove to the outskirts of Payton, where JanCo was located in an isolated, wooded area, Nadia refined her plan. It could be done, she realized, and without much trouble. Everything she needed was in the lab.

They pulled up to the employee parking lot entrance. Peter rolled down his window and stuck a plastic card into the slot, and the gate opened. He'd taken her card from her purse, she realized.

"How will Denise get in?"

Peter didn't answer, but he still wore that smug smile, so clearly he'd planned for this ahead of time. He pulled his car into a spot in the very back of the lot.

It was close to five o'clock, when most employees clocked out. Soon most of the cars in the packed lot would be gone. But there were always a few left. Many of JanCo's scientists and technicians worked odd hours. Contrary to what Nadia had told Peter, no new security measures had been instituted, no 8:00 p.m. curfew. Employees could and did work in their labs until all hours. No one would notice Peter's car or think it strange.

"You have thirty minutes," Peter said.

"That's not enough—"

"Of course it's enough. The samples are already made up—you forget, I know something about how the nano lab operates, thanks to your loose lips. You could do it in ten minutes. I'm being generous because I don't want you to appear rushed. Everyone must think you're simply there to catch up on work you've missed while you were out sick."

That was exactly what they would think. Nadia rarely took time off. She was responsible about deadlines and timelines, and she didn't like to inconvenience other members of her team by not delivering work when promised. She often stayed late when she got behind.

"What if someone sees me?"

"No one will question you. It's your project."

"How will I explain the missing sample? Inventory controls are very tight."

"That will not be my problem. You of course will do nothing to implicate me, or Lily will never be safe. Not so long as I walk this earth. Should I be arrested, it will not end your problems. I have many friends with long arms."

Nadia shivered. She'd told Rex that early on—that so long as Peter lived, even incarcerated, he was a threat. "That's just it," she said softly. "If I give you the Petro-Nano, and you turn it over to the wrong people, none of us will be walking this earth, because the earth will be a cold, dead rock."

"You must think I work for idiots."

"I think you work for desperate people. If they do not win the dangerous game they're playing, if they see they are about to fail in their goals, they will not hesitate to destroy everyone along with themselves."

"That is American propaganda talking," Peter said. "The men I work for know what they're doing. The only way to stop American imperialism from destroying the earth is to balance the power. I am helping them to balance power, Nadia."

"If you believe that, you're a bigger fool than I thought."

His face tensed, and she thought for a moment he was going to hit her again. But he didn't. He relaxed and flashed that smug smile. "You cannot provoke me. I have won, darling." He opened the glove compartment and pulled out her ID badge, which he'd also apparently retrieved from her purse. He looped the chain around her neck. Then he produced a silver ballpoint pen from the glove compartment and clipped it to the collar of her sweater.

"This is the microphone," he said. "It is very sensitive, picks up your conversation as well as any around you. If you attempt to remove it, I will be able to tell, so don't.

"And don't think you can signal anyone without speaking. Remember, you can turn me in. But you do not know where Denise and Lily are. And if any cop cars show up, if anyone approaches this car, if anything out of the ordinary happens—*anything*—Denise will do exactly as she promised. If you do not return in the allotted time, Lily will die in a most unpleasant manner. I think Denise is actually hoping something will go wrong. She enjoys torture, and she is surprisingly good at it."

Nadia fixed her gaze on her ex-husband, and it must have been as hard and cold as she meant it to be, because Peter's smile died on his lips.

"If anything happens to my child, I will hunt you, and I will find you. And if you kill me, there are others behind me. The bounty hunter is a former marine sniper who will not think twice about shooting you between the eyes." She did not have anything to lose by telling Peter now, she reasoned. She wanted him to know fear. If he got away from here, she wanted him looking over his shoulder, terrified—until Rex found him.

Rex would find him, and then Peter would wish he'd never been born.

"The clock has started," Peter said, just as steely. "You are wasting time."

Nadia got out and walked briskly toward the main entrance to JanCo Labs, going over in her mind what she would do once she reached her lab. She wondered if there was any way she could ditch the wire without Peter knowing. Could he really tell if she removed it?

She was afraid to try it.

She entered through the heavy glass doors and into a well-appointed lobby dominated by a huge front desk. Lonnie, JanCo's longtime receptionist, presided over the lobby, looking deceptively harmless. But she was former air force, trained in all kinds of weapons, and behind that desk she was armed to the teeth. She smiled at Nadia, recognizing her. Nadia smiled back and inserted her magnetic badge into the reader near a steel door. The door slid open, and Nadia entered.

She walked along the familiar maze of sterile white corridors. On the way, she passed one of the security guards. "Hi, Tim." She tried to act as normally as possible. Now that she had committed to her plan, she did not want anyone to stop her. And they *would* stop her. But the more she thought about it, the more she realized her plan was the only way.

If she summoned authorities, Lily would die.

If she delivered a fake sample of the Petro-Nano, Peter would discover she'd duped him, and Lily would die.

No, her way was the only way to save her daughter's life.

The nano lab was on the basement level, a level dug into solid limestone. She took the stairs rather than waiting for the elevator. At the bottom of the stairs she pushed through another heavy metal door, walked down another corridor. The hallways seemed strangely quiet to her.

Another security guard was stationed just outside the nano lab. Normally it was the same guy, Lars. She started to greet him when she realized it wasn't Lars at all.

Rex was standing there, dressed in a JanCo Security Force uniform of black pants and a white shirt. She cursed silently, torn by conflicting emotions at the sight of him. She felt relieved that she was no longer fighting against Peter alone—Rex was here, he wanted to rescue her, rescue Lily, bring Peter to justice. But she was also upset that he'd violated the confidence she'd placed in him. Clearly he'd told someone—probably Robert Candless, JanCo's Chief of Security—about what he perceived as a threat to not only national security, but world order.

Damn it. *Damn it!* He should have trusted her. Did he think she would actually turn over a hazardous substance to a terrorist when she'd promised him she wouldn't?

"H-hi, Lars," she said, signaling frantically that she was wired.

He nodded. "Hello, Dr. Penn. Haven't seen you in a couple of days."

"I had some kind of stomach thing, but I'm better now. I thought I'd catch up on some work."

"Sure thing."

She reached the door leading to the nano lab, Rex at her heels. Entrance required not only her magnetic badge, but an iris scan as well. Unless things had been changed, Rex wouldn't be able to follow her into the lab—nor did she want him to.

"I'm really far behind," she said. "But I'm sure I'll have everything under control soon." She gave him the "okay" hand signal, placed her right eye in front of the iris scanner, and waited to be admitted through the first of two sets of doors. If Rex tried to follow her, the pressure-sensitive floor between the two doors would detect his presence, and the second doors would not open.

He didn't try to follow her. She entered the lab alone.

A couple of her co-workers were there, scientists who were running their own nano projects, and two lab technicians. They all greeted Nadia with surprise.

"What are you doing here?" asked Dick Haney.

She gave them the same speech she'd given Rex, and asked if anything was going on that she needed to know about.

"No, it's been pretty quiet," said Dick. Everyone soon returned to whatever tasks they'd been absorbed in before her arrival, leading her to believe they did not know what was going on. But that was how Robert Candless would handle it. He would inform employees of the security risk only on a need-to-know basis.

Left to her own devices, Nadia quickly got to work. She had everything here in the lab that she would need—cyanide salts and some hydrochloric acid. The phone rang. She let someone else get it.

"Nadia?" It was one of the technicians. "For you."

Panic rose in her throat. Should she take the call? Would Peter think she was betraying him? "Can you take a message?" Nadia asked. "I just walked in the door. I need to catch my breath."

As she donned a white lab coat over her street clothes, she heard the technician murmuring into the phone. Then he was talking to Nadia again. "It's the guy from requisitions," he said. "He's called about ten times already. He needs to know something about ribonucleic acid you ordered—"

"All right, I'll take it." Then she whispered, "Peter, I'm answering the phone. They'll think it odd if I don't. I won't say anything to give you away." She picked up an extension near her and put it to her right ear, farthest from the microphone. "Nadia Penn speaking."

"It's Rex."

"Yes, Mr. Perkins."

"You can just answer yes or no. Is Peter on the lab premises?"

"Yes, that's right. But you mustn't send the sample now—I'm not ready for it. I've been out a couple of days and I'm behind schedule." Did Rex understand what she was saying?

"You don't want us to move in?"

"No, I don't. But it sounds like everything is under control."

"Is Lily still in danger?"

"Yes, that's right. But it won't be too long." Could he trust her? She knew what had to be done, and she could do it. "Please, just put that order on hold," she said. "I'll call you when I'm ready for it."

"You won't be allowed to leave the building," Rex said.

"Oh, yes, I will. Thank you so much. I appreciate your patience. It will all work out. Bye, now." She hung up before she thought of anything else inane to say. She would be very lucky if Peter hadn't caught on to the fact she was giving someone signals over the phone.

As she'd talked with the phone tucked between her shoulder and her ear, she'd been assembling the ingredients she would need, and also a very special container that would allow her to dump the cyanide salts into a small beaker of HCl simply by removing the top. She rigged up something that looked complex, something that Peter would believe held the real Petro-Nano. In reality, the contents of the beaker would be deadly, but not for billions of people—just for one. The moment the cyanide salts hit the acid, hydrocyanic acid fumes would rise from the beaker. One good whiff would kill a human being in seconds.

She'd thought about using it to kill Peter. But chances were, he wouldn't open the beaker here. He would take it to someone who could verify the contents. And even if he did open it now, nothing would be accomplished by killing Peter. Denise would see what had happened and make good on her threat.

So Nadia had come up with another idea. She would inhale the cyanide fumes herself. She would kill herself as Peter looked on, horrified and helpless to stop her.

A dead woman couldn't be blackmailed, or manipulated in any way. After he realized she was dead, he would know his plan to get the Petro-Nano was just as dead. No purpose would be served in harming Lily— he would harm Lily only to hurt Nadia.

Furthermore, murdering a child would turn him into a baby-killer, which would only intensify the manhunt. No, his best interests would be served if he released Lily and fled. Once the child was found safe, the incentive to find Peter would drop considerably. Without a hostage or a weapon of mass destruction, he was hardly worth chasing down.

She could only hope Peter was smart enough to figure that out.

Chapter Thirteen

Rex disconnected the phone. Robert Candless and Ace had listened in on the conversation. They were in a small "situation room" set up for any type of security breach. It came complete with secure, encrypted phones and enough weapons to arm a small revolution.

"She was trying to tell us she has everything under control," Rex said. "She has a plan."

"A plan to sell out, you mean," Candless said. The security director was a fireplug of a man with a loud, grating voice, a shaved head and a God complex. Rex hadn't liked the guy from the moment they met. Ace had said he was former CIA, reason enough not to trust him.

"No," Rex argued. "She won't give Peter anything dangerous. She didn't tell me what Peter wanted," Rex lied, "but she told me it was too dangerous to put into the hands of a madman."

"To put it mildly," Candless said. "Nadia is a good person, don't get me wrong. But her child's life is at stake. I don't expect a mother to behave rationally."

Rex fixed Candless with a steely glare. "Nadia is rational. She will not put innocent lives in danger. My guess is she'll deliver a phony sample to Peter, to buy some time."

Candless made a sound of disgust. "She's a woman, and she just spent almost twenty-four hours with her ex-husband. You don't think he put the moves on her? I hate to be sexist, but women are vulnerable to their emotions. If Peter made her believe he still loves her, that he's really one of the good guys, all bets are off. He could have appealed to her Russian heritage. He could have offered to cut her in on the payment he's undoubtedly getting for this little job. He could have convinced her they would return to Russia and live like royalty."

Rex shook his head. "She's not that stupid. He kidnapped her child. He threatened to cut off her ear. Nadia isn't going to forgive him that."

"We can't take the risk."

Rex wanted to argue the case further. He'd spent only a few days with Nadia, but he felt he knew her better than any human on earth. She would not cave in to Peter's demands. Not even to save Lily. But before he could try again to convince Candless to give Nadia her head, a phone rang and Candless grabbed it.

"Candless here." He listened, tense, as Rex and Ace held their collective breath. "We're on it." He hung up and looked at the other two men. "My men have reviewed the surveillance video. Nadia entered the JanCo employee parking lot in the passenger seat of a gold 1994 Lincoln Town Car. The man driving looks like our Russkie. No one else in the car. The car is now parked in the lot. The man is still there. I'll send some men in to take him. Then give me ten minutes with him. He'll tell us where the kid is."

Rex couldn't believe the depth of this guy's ego—or his stupidity. "If it was that easy, Nadia would have just told us where he was the moment she walked in."

"The microphone—"

"She would have written it down. There's a reason she doesn't want him taken, and I think it has to do with her daughter. She'll never get her daughter back if his plans go south at this point."

"Just what do you suggest?" Candless asked with a sneer.

"Let someone from my team go in and do something to his car. That way if he tries to drive away, he won't get far."

"Nadia is still not leaving the building."

"I didn't say she had to. Just don't tip Peter Danilov off. Not yet."

"Our guys can do it," Ace added. "We can disable the car without his ever knowing."

Candless sighed. "Where's your team? I'll have to try to get them on the property without Danilov seeing them."

"Oh, they're already here," Rex said easily. The shock in Candless's eyes was almost funny, and Rex would laugh about it later—after Nadia and Lily were safe. "Your security sucks." And it did. It had been simple enough to smuggle Craig and Lori beneath the cargo cover of Rex's Blazer. Chances were his two team members had already spotted Peter. But they wouldn't move until he gave them the go-ahead.

Beau and Gavin were outside the JanCo perimeter fence, scouring the surrounding woods and farmlands for signs of Peter's co-conspirators. Peter would probably have someone on the outside, ready to warn him if law enforcement was approaching.

Candless's mouth thinned while Ace tried not to laugh. "Give your people the go-ahead to contain Danilov however they see fit. But if he escapes, I'm holding you personally responsible."

Rex made a quick call to Craig on the encrypted cell phones they were all using. Candless had come up with a dozen of the things after declaring the headset radios too vulnerable to eavesdropping.

"Did you spot Peter?" Rex asked.

"He's in a gold Lincoln Town Car. All alone, just sitting there with a smug look on his face."

"Disable his car."

"Not a problem," Craig said.

IN THE LAB, NADIA WAS ready to leave. The suicide cocktail was tucked into her inside jacket pocket. But she had to do one more very important thing. She tore a page out of one of her lab notebooks and, always conscious of the time ticking away, scribbled out a note to Lily, explaining why she'd killed herself and expressing her love in embarrassing, flowery excess. She debated, then added a note to Rex: "I love you for trying to save me and Lily."

She thought for a moment, then added, "I love you because you're you." She found she no longer blamed him for betraying her trust. If he wanted even a chance at recovering her and Lily, he needed Robert Candless's cooperation. There were many things she wanted to say, but she didn't have time. She folded the note, left it on the counter and headed for the exit.

As she expected, Rex and Candless were waiting for her, but they said nothing. Instead, Rex handed her an open notebook. On the first page he'd scribbled, "You can't go back out. It's too dangerous."

"I'm on my way out," she said aloud, for Peter's benefit as well as the two men now flanking her as she made her way down the hall. "I know I'm close to the deadline, but please be patient. I've been gone for three days and people want to talk to me. I will try to extricate myself as quickly as possible." She reasoned that if Peter thought she was making a good-faith effort to follow his instructions, he wouldn't order Denise to begin the finger-lopping.

As she walked, she scribbled her own note to Rex: "I am not giving him anything dangerous. It's a fake."

She felt, rather than saw, Candless tense beside her. He grabbed the notebook and wrote, "I can't take that chance."

She stopped in front of the elevator this time, rather than the stairs, to buy her just a few more seconds. She took the notebook and scribbled back, "You don't trust me?"

The elevator arrived, the doors opened. She stepped inside with the two men. Rex grabbed the notebook. "Yes, we trust you. Can't risk your safety."

She grabbed the notebook and pen, quietly turned to a fresh page. "You stop me, you kill my daughter." She let both men read it. Then she observed their faces. She saw regret in Rex's eyes—regret that he was going to have to let Lily die? And in Robert Candless's coarse, blunt features, she saw distrust. He still did not believe her.

He was not going to let her leave.

She wondered if she could get his gun away. Oh, Lord, what was she thinking? Candless was ex-CIA. Her skills with a gun extended only to target practice. She had no practical experience, only a head full of stories and advice from her KGB grandma.

As they exited the elevator, Nadia noted that the corridor was completely empty. The lab had a safe room, on the basement level, in case of an environmental disaster or a terrorist attack. It was large enough to house every employee in the building. Concrete walls surrounded by limestone, an air filtration system, food and water—like an old-fashioned bomb shelter from the 1950s. Nadia wondered if everyone had been shepherded there as a safety precaution.

As they neared the front entrance, all of them in a tense truce, Candless made his move. He took her arm, almost gently. "I'm sorry, Dr. Penn. Nadia. I know you love your daughter, and I'm sorry she's been put at risk. But I can't let you leave—"

Nadia shoved an elbow into his soft midsection and wiggled out of his grasp, then ran for the exit. Had it been locked down? Could it be locked down? She thought the security precautions at JanCo were mostly designed to keep people out, not in.

"Stop or I'll shoot!" Candless's voice was sharp, deadly.

She stopped. She didn't doubt for a minute that he would kill her. She turned and saw that he had his 9 mm pointed at her head. Rex stood next to him, a look of disbelief, then anguish on his face.

"On the floor," Candless ordered.

She should run for it. She was going to die anyway. If Peter saw her die in a fiery spray of bullets as she was attempting to run out the door, wouldn't it serve the same purpose as her planned method of suicide?

Then something amazing happened. In a movement so quick it was a blur, Rex took Robert Candless's gun away. One minute, the security director was pointing his weapon at Nadia; the next, he was on his knees with one arm twisted behind him, completely under Rex's control.

Now Rex had *his* gun pointed at Nadia.

"You can't shoot me," she said. "You can't shoot a woman." It was unspeakably cruel for her to allude to his painful past. But she had to get out that door. Just a few more feet.

"I will shoot you, Nadia," he said, his voice full of regret.

"Then why did you take Candless's gun away?"

"Because I was afraid he would go for your head. I'll incapacitate you, but I won't kill you."

She pulled the small beaker out of her lab coat. Candless knew of the Petro-Nano's potential, but he wasn't a scientist. He had no way of recognizing the fact that what she held wasn't the real thing. He wouldn't know a Petro-Nano from peanut butter. "You know what I have here, right?" she said to Rex. He wouldn't be able to recognize the Petro-Nano, either. But she hoped that he knew her well enough to know she was playacting for Peter's benefit. "You put the gun down right now, or I will open this beaker—"

"Shoot her," Candless said. "For God's sake, Bettencourt, you have no idea what you're dealing with. That substance could kill billions of people!"

"If you shoot me," she said, "I'll drop the beaker and it will break. Bad news for everyone."

"HOW ABOUT WE LET THE AIR out of his tires?" Craig suggested. He and Lori were hiding behind a huge Suburban, watching Peter's car through two layers of tinted auto glass.

"He'll hear it," she said. "We'd do better to cut the gas line. It would serve our purposes to have him drive at least a little way, maybe lead us closer to Nadia's baby."

"Do you know how to cut a gas line?"

Lori gave him a sideways look. "Don't you?"

She scared him, sometimes. "So how do we approach his car without being seen?"

"I have an idea." Lori had brought a small duffel bag with her, and from it she produced a slim-jim, a thin strip of metal used to unlock car doors from the outside.

"You know it's illegal to own those, don't you?"

"What? It's a piece of an old metal ruler. Nothing illegal about that." She slid the device against the window of the Suburban and in moments had popped the lock. Craig steeled himself for an alarm to go off, but it didn't.

"I never saw this. I'm looking up at the clouds." At least the weather had cleared. It was cold, but no longer raining. "How did you know the car didn't have an alarm?"

"One of the rear windows is cracked open. No one sets a car alarm, then leaves a window open." She yanked the Suburban's door open, then briefly rummaged around in the back until she produced a skateboard. "I saw this through the window. I'm going to use it like a mechanic's creeper. I'll slide under cars until I reach Peter's. There's no chance he'll see me."

"You're not going," Craig corrected her. "Rex will kill me. I'm supposed to be keeping you safe and out of trouble."

It was the wrong thing to say to Lori, and he knew it the moment the words were out of his mouth. She hated it when her brother tried to protect her.

"I'm smaller than you," she said as she put the skateboard down, then lay on top of it, chest down. She could slide under the Suburban, though she would never make it under cars with a lower ground clearance.

Fortunately, this was Texas, where most people drove SUVs or pickup trucks, whether they needed the hauling capacity or not.

Craig knew he wouldn't be able to stop her short of bodily throwing himself on top of her. Then their assignment wouldn't get done.

"I'll cover you," he said, intending to follow by crouching down and darting from car to car.

"It's a race," she said with a grin, then started off.

He soon found that she'd been right—her method was highly preferable to his. He had to duckwalk or crawl from behind one car to the next, leaving himself vulnerable. When he was about halfway there, he stopped. There was too great a chance that Peter could spot him, which would put their entire operation in danger. Much as he hated it, he had to let Lori go it alone. He was close enough to provide cover if Peter did spot her.

PETER DIDN'T LIKE his chances. As he listened through his earphone to the drama unfolding just past the lobby of JanCo labs, he felt sick to his stomach. Nadia had done everything he asked of her, but it hadn't been enough. Someone else in the lab must have seen her stealing the Petro-Nano and reported her to security. She'd warned him that something like that could happen, and she'd been right.

Though Peter had spent most of the past few months despising Nadia for being the obstinate barrier to his ultimate goal, right now he was in awe of her bravery. A lesser woman would have crumbled, given up and tossed Peter to the wolves. But she was so determined to save her baby's life, she was going to the wall.

He wished he hadn't had to pressure her into this. He wished she truly understood what he was trying to do. He had no desire to destroy the world. He wanted to save the world from total United States domination. A world dictator, that was what the future held, unless someone did something.

He was that someone.

He would not have killed her baby. But he'd led her to believe he was a monster. It was the only way he'd been able to convince her he meant business.

He felt uncomfortable sitting in the car. Earlier, it had seemed safe enough. He'd been that sure of Nadia's cooperation. Now, though, the situation was volatile. If Nadia succeeded in getting out the door, she would run straight for his car, and he would be a sitting duck. Candless had undoubtedly notified security of the risk, and sharpshooters might even now be searching the parking lot for Peter.

Trying to look casual, he got out of the car, as if he was just heading into work after an early dinner break. He wore his old JanCo badge around his neck. As he walked between two vans, he ducked down. From here, he had a perfect view of the front entrance, and he could also keep an eye on his car in case it had been identified through the video surveillance at the front gate.

What he needed now was another car. Too bad he did not know how to steal one. That had been one of Denise's specialties.

He was currently out of contact with Denise. Despite what he'd told Nadia, she was not observing from a vantage point. It would have been too easy for her to be spotted and apprehended. And Lily was his one ace-in-the-hole. Denise and the baby were two miles away at a fast-food restaurant with their getaway vehicle. But if he did not show up within the hour, she would flee the country without him.

She might not kill Lily—he wasn't really sure how cruel Denise was. At the very least, though, Denise would take Lily to Russia. So even though Nadia was doing her best to give Peter what he'd asked her for, she would never see her daughter again. It was a shame, really. But sometimes, sacrifice was necessary for the greater good.

AS HE HELD THE GUN pointed at Nadia, Rex weighed his options. He could shoot Nadia. Chances were good the beaker wouldn't break. The glass they used for scientific purposes was strong stuff.

He could continue to try to talk her into surrendering. But he recognized that belligerent look in her eye. She was not a woman on the verge of compromise. This was all or nothing.

"You can't shoot me," she repeated. "You love me."

He did. He did love her. His finger tightened against the trigger, but he could not make himself squeeze hard enough to send a bullet ripping into Nadia's body. He'd been right all along; he was ruined. He could no longer kill, not even when the fate of the world was at stake.

She must have seen the indecision there, because she turned and ran out the door.

"You idiot!" Candless screamed. "Do you have any idea what you've just done?"

Rex took a deep breath, and suddenly he saw things clearly. And yes, he did realize what he'd done. He'd put his trust in Nadia, a trust that never should have wavered in the first place. He'd surrendered control to her. Because he loved her, and he knew her, and she wasn't a selfish fool. He hadn't hesitated because he lacked the *cojones* to kill.

"She doesn't have the Petro-Nano," Rex said as he used a phone cord to tie Candless's hands and feet, knowing now he was right. He hadn't killed her because on some level he knew she wouldn't cut off her nose to spite her face. She wouldn't risk wiping out the planet to save her daughter's life. She was stronger than that.

Yes, twice before she'd behaved irrationally where Lily was concerned. But not this time.

NADIA EXITED JanCo Labs and walked purposefully across the parking lot toward Peter's car. She expected to hear the crack of rifle fire, feel the bullet gouging her flesh or exploding her skull. It wouldn't matter, so long as Peter witnessed it. But it didn't happen. She was being allowed to continue.

No telling what Peter thought of the dialogue he'd just overheard. Did he still think he could get away with the Petro-Nano? If everyone truly believed Nadia had the means for world destruction in the pocket of her lab coat, perhaps they were so paralyzed with fright that they would make no move to stop either one of them.

It was possible that was what Peter believed.

As she approached Peter's car, she realized something was wrong. The car was empty. She drew closer still, but he was nowhere in sight.

Had he been quietly taken into custody? Was he, even now, spilling his guts, telling them where to find Lily?

"Peter?" she called out. "I'm here, at the car. I have what you want. You can get away. They're so scared, they won't stop you."

Nothing.

"Peter, please, where are you?" How could she carry out her plan if he wasn't there to witness it?

Someone grabbed her from behind. One arm went around her neck in a headlock; the other grabbed her arm and bent it behind her. She was wrestled to the pavement, shielded from view by several large vehicles.

Peter. Though he hadn't made a sound, she knew the feel of him, the smell of him.

"This isn't necessary," she said, trying to sound calm while in reality panic engulfed her. He pinned her on her back with a knee to her already bruised ribs. "For God's sake, you must be insane! You could have broken the beaker."

"Where is it?"

"In my lab coat. Let me—"

"Don't move!" He reached inside her lab coat and pulled out the beaker containing her suicide cocktail. His grin was maniacal as he gazed on what he thought was his prize, his long-sought treasure.

"I have to show you how to handle the sample," Nadia said desperately, still trying to salvage her plan. "The beaker has to be opened in a special way or the whole thing could be ruined."

"Our scientists are not stupid," Peter said.

Abruptly he removed his knee from her solar plexus and stood. She tried to follow suit, but the large handgun he pointed at her heart halted her. The gun had a silencer, too.

"Peter, I've done everything you asked. I don't know how Robert Candless found out. Someone must have seen me acting suspiciously. I was so nervous! But I won't turn you in. You can get away if you leave now. Just tell me where Lily is."

"I'll take you to her. You're coming with me. Now get up."

The last time Peter had promised to take Nadia to her child, he'd been lying. She had no reason to believe him now. "You want me to be your hostage, your shield so you can get out of here. You'll kill me as soon as you're clear."

"I won't kill you," he said, but she saw how he averted his eyes and realized he was lying.

"You have no choice but to kill me," Nadia countered.

"I won't go with you. You'll have to kill me now. Then you'll have to run for your life. Because, Peter? That beaker you're holding doesn't contain the Petro-Nano. It's harmless water and baking powder."

"I don't believe you. They wouldn't have tried to stop you if you didn't have the real thing. They would have shot me by now if this wasn't the real thing. Now they're too afraid."

"I won't come with you. Without me to worry about, Rex will shoot you in the head before you can clear the parking lot."

"Then why hasn't he done it already?" Peter asked smugly.

"Because you have a gun pointed at me. He doesn't want to get me killed."

"Get up! Or I'll shoot you in the knee! I will torture your child!"

He was desperate now, and Nadia knew she'd finally outmaneuvered him. Resigned to her fate, she merely stared up at him from the ground. She could not save Lily now—and maybe there'd never been that chance.

"Why, Peter?" This would probably be her last chance. Not the final confrontation she'd had in mind, but she had to play with the hand she'd been dealt. "I thought you were smarter than this. You're just going to get yourself killed."

"I would gladly die to destroy America. If it comes to that, they'll write about me in the history books."

She had her answer, then. He wanted to matter, to be important.

Peter straightened his arm and took aim. "I should

shoot you in the head. You'd die faster. But I can't bring myself to ruin your pretty face. See, I'm not really a heartless monster."

Where was Rex? Nadia wondered wildly. Did he actually believe she'd delivered the Petro-Nano? Was that why Rex hadn't taken Peter down, because he was afraid Peter would drop the beaker and annihilate the earth? Or was he really concerned about her welfare?

In an instinctual effort to save herself, Nadia tried to roll under the nearest car. But she wasn't fast enough. Peter pulled the trigger.

Searing pain sliced through Nadia's chest. She could not move or think or do anything except acknowledge the terrible pain. The bullet's impact knocked the breath out of her, and she struggled desperately to get some oxygen into her lungs.

Peter cursed. She was vaguely aware of the sound of a car's motor starting, tires screeching. She looked up at the clear blue winter sky and silently said goodbye to Lily and her mother…and Rex. Everyone she loved.

Chapter Fourteen

Before that first shot, Rex had exited JanCo labs and sprinted across the open part of the parking lot. He saw Peter grab Nadia, but by the time he'd maneuvered into a position where he had a clear shot, he couldn't take it—Peter had a gun pointed at Nadia. He couldn't see Nadia, but he knew she was on the ground. If he killed Peter now, there was a good chance the Russian would tense as the bullet found its mark, causing the trigger to release. And Nadia would be dead.

If he waited, Peter might get in his car and drive off, leaving Nadia to survive—and leading them to Lily. In a few fractions of a second, Rex considered whether Peter would pull the trigger. He put himself inside the target's head, as he'd been trained to do. If Peter were rational, he would realize it wouldn't serve his purpose to kill Nadia. He would take her as a hostage.

Rex's secure cell phone rang and he debated whether to answer it. Then he recognized the ring as belonging to Ace—they each had a coded ring—and decided he'd better explain himself.

"What the hell is going on here?" Ace's voice came

over the radio. "What is Robert Candless doing trussed up like a pig on its way to market?"

"He was going to kill Nadia," Rex returned.

"Where is Nadia? Where are you? Where is Peter?"

Rex described the situation as quickly and calmly as he could.

"Do you think he'll kill her?"

"Not unless she forces the—" The muffled report of a gun cut him off. In a purely instinctual reaction, Rex pulled the trigger of his Glock. But he was at least thirty yards away, too far for an accurate shot with a handgun, and for the first time in his career, he missed his target altogether. Peter, alert to the threat, had ducked the moment he squeezed the trigger and dived into his car.

Rex, in a firestorm of emotion, fired three more times. He hit the car, shattering glass. But apparently he did not hit Peter, because Peter screeched out of his parking place. Then reason took over, and Rex held his fire. Peter could not lead them to Lily if he was dead.

Running toward where he thought Nadia was, Rex yelled into the cell phone. "Ace, call for medical help. I think Nadia's injured." As for the rest of his team, he wished now they had their trusty headset radios. But he had to believe that the other team members were watching and knew what to do.

He heard another car engine start; it sounded like his Blazer.

Nadia was maybe twenty yards away now, but it was the longest twenty yards Rex had ever run, dodging around cars. When he reached the spot where he'd seen Peter knock her to the ground, the sight that greeted him froze his blood. Nadia lay on her back, still as a painting. Her pristine white lab coat and the sweater beneath it were stained bright crimson.

Rex fell to his knees beside Nadia. "Oh, God. Oh, Jesus, please, no." But just then he heard a shuddering breath, and he realized Nadia was still alive. Her skin was almost as white as her coat, but her eyelids fluttered open.

Alive, and conscious. No blood seeped out from beneath her, meaning the bullet had probably not gone straight through her and exited out her back. She could be bleeding internally. He ripped her shirt open and pressed his hands against the entrance wound, which was just under her right breast, and did his best to stanch the flow of blood.

"G-get…" she started, but Rex hushed her.

"Don't try to talk."

"H-have to…didn't give him…it's…it's…" Her voice was a thready whisper, and he leaned closer to hear her. "…it's cyanide. Lethal fumes."

Rex understood instantly. The beaker wouldn't lead to mass death, but it might kill one—or two.

"Lily. Save my daughter," Nadia said, her voice slightly stronger, though her breathing was labored and painful to hear. "Leave me. Get Lily. Save her."

The paramedics weren't far away. When the First Strike team had planned this venture with Robert Candless, they'd made sure emergency response vehicles would be close at hand.

Paramedics had to bodily pull Rex away from Nadia. Then they swarmed on her like locusts, hooking her up with IVs and oxygen and stuff Rex didn't recognize. But they looked reassuringly competent, shouting at each other using incomprehensible medical jargon.

Ace joined him. "Lori said Peter won't get far. They cut his fuel line."

"I want him to get away," Rex said. "I want him to lead us to Lily." It was the only thing that mattered now. Rex had failed Nadia at the crucial moment. He'd hesitated, believing Peter wouldn't kill her. Granted, it had been a bad judgment call, not a loss of nerve.

He made contact with Lori on the cell phone. "When his car quits, Peter will take off on foot. Do not take him down. Follow him, but let him think he's gotten away. And let's change over to the radios. These cell phones suck." He wanted to be able to speak to everyone at once—and hear them instantly if they spotted something.

"What if Peter does get away?" Ace asked. "Candless said what's in that test tube could—"

"It's harmless except to the one person who opens it," Rex said, heading at a run for Ace's Jeep Cherokee, which they'd parked in the employee lot earlier today in case they needed extra transportation. "Nadia told me."

"You're sure?" Ace asked, keeping pace. He was more than twenty years Rex's senior, but he wasn't even winded.

"Absolutely." He spoke into the phone again.

Ace nodded. "That's good enough for me."

PETER GOT A COUPLE OF MILES away from JanCo before his car sputtered and died. But he wouldn't have gotten much farther anyway. One of the bullets that had come flying his way had nicked a tire, and now it was flat.

With a muffled curse, he stuffed the precious beaker into a secret compartment in his padded backpack, which he'd modified especially for that purpose. Then he donned a baseball cap festooned with fake, long gray hair, wincing a bit at the unexpected pain. He reached up and realized he was bleeding. Had flying glass cut his head? Well, it couldn't be too bad. He quickly pressed on a false mustache and a pair of wire-rimmed glasses.

Now he was just an old hippie out for a winter hike.

He abandoned the car on the side of the highway and scaled a small fence. Beyond the fence were acres and acres of piney woods, great cover. They wouldn't be able to spot him from a helicopter. They could track him with dogs, but it would take them a long time to get dogs to the area.

Amazingly, he hadn't been followed as he'd crashed through the JanCo gates. They were too scared, now that they knew the power he wielded. He'd seen only one other car on the road, a black Mustang, and it had passed him without a second glance.

The strip shopping center where Denise awaited him was just on the other side of this patch of woods, about a mile away. He was in excellent shape, and the slight wound on his scalp wouldn't slow him down at all. He expected to reach his destination in twenty minutes, which would be just under Denise's deadline. They would calmly climb into Denise's recently stolen silver BMW—he'd requested that she get them a nice car for their final run to the private airstrip, where a twin-engine Cessna awaited them. The Cessna would take them to another airport, where a Learjet, on legitimate business to Turkey with all permits and passports in order, would take them out of this cursed country.

He hoped never to see American soil again.

"WE'VE SPOTTED HIM," came Beau's voice over the headset. "He's trucking through the woods at a good pace. Gavin and I are on it. Over."

"Where's your car?" Rex said. "I need it."

Beau explained where the Mustang was parked, keys under the seat, as they'd planned earlier.

So far so good, Rex thought, trying to keep his mind on his work and away from the mental image of Nadia lying on the pavement covered in her own blood. He had already let his feelings for her distract him, cloud his judgment. But maybe, just maybe, missing Peter had been a good thing. Killing him wouldn't bring Nadia back. Letting him live, though, might save Lily's life.

A minute later, he and Ace passed the disabled gold Lincoln on the side of the road. Beau's black Mustang was about a half mile farther. "Beau, what direction is the target moving?" Rex asked into the radio.

"Due south," Beau responded. "He seems to have an agenda."

Ace consulted the satellite maps. "Looks like there's a big shopping center on the other side of this hill. Also an old logging road that cuts through roughly the spine of the hill."

"Lori, Craig, what's your twenty?" Rex asked.

"Look straight ahead, bro," said Lori. Sure enough, his own Blazer was coming straight at them. He'd left it parked outside the JanCo security gates, anticipating the need for more vehicles. "We drove on past when he pulled off the road—didn't want him to see us stop. We were coming on foot from a different angle when we heard Beau say they'd spotted him."

As Lori jumped out of the Blazer, she gasped, her gaze riveted on her brother. "Whose blood?"

"Nadia's."

Her face tensed with worry. "We heard the shot, but we couldn't see what happened. Is she…?"

"I don't know," Rex said curtly as he spread the satellite map over the hood of his car. "Craig, I want you to check out this logging road. Denise might be waiting somewhere along there. But if he's merely crossing that road, let him go. If you find nothing, go next to this shopping center. Ace and I will already be there. Lori, you take Beau's Mustang and follow us. We'll all look for Lily. Failing that, a well-groomed woman with a face like a rat."

"They might not be there," Ace pointed out. "Denise and Lily might be halfway to Russia by now."

"Peter must have support nearby. If it's not Denise, it's someone else. Be ready to tail whoever it is."

"Rex." Lori laid a hand on her brother's arm. "Does Peter have—did he get what he was looking for?" No one but Rex knew what that something was, but they all knew of the potential danger.

"No. But he's got a bottle full of cyanide, so watch out. The fumes can kill you."

As HE APPROACHED the logging road that roughly bisected this section of woods, Peter slowed, taking the opportunity to catch his breath and listen. Car engines, helicopters, voices—they carried on the wind. But he heard nothing. Apparently his enemies were giving him wide berth.

He hoped they hadn't found Denise. She was expendable, but he'd come to like her over the past few weeks they'd been planning and working together. At first he'd been worried when the organization had assigned him a woman partner. But he'd soon found out she was worthy. Cunning and vicious, not to mention skillful in bed. Then there was the added bonus that a woman could be forced to care for the child, something he hadn't looked forward to. Another man would never have been coerced into changing diapers.

He knew exactly where he would emerge from the woods. He had planned for this contingency, a chase on foot. He had studied the terrain. From his emergence point, he would see whether the BMW was parked in the proper spot, whether Denise was behind the wheel. She would be eating a fast-food meal and reading a women's magazine, but she would be watching for him. And she would signal him if the coast was clear. He would work his way down from the slight incline and across the road to the parking lot, climb in, and they would be off.

There was the matter of Lily. Once they escaped, authorities would be looking for a couple with a baby. Her pictures would be all over the media. They would have to get rid of her.

Abandonment would be their best bet. Now that Nadia was dead, there would be no satisfaction for either of them in carrying out his threat, even though she'd tried, at the last minute, to deceive him. In fact, they could just leave Lily at the side of the road someplace. They could even use her as a false clue, make the authorities think they were heading one direction, then double back and go a different way.

Stupid cops, or bounty hunters, or whoever they were. They'd never catch him. By the time they put together a plan for stopping what they saw as a new terrorism threat, the man they were looking for would no longer exist.

The logging road was quiet, abandoned. There was a fresh set of tire tracks in the mud, but he imagined kids came up here joyriding in their SUVs all the time. There was no one here now.

He hitched his pack up higher onto his shoulders and resumed his progress through the woods, accelerating once again into an easy lope.

REX WAS APPALLED when he got his first close-up look at the shopping center. It was huge. He knew aerial photographs were deceiving that way, but he hadn't envisioned such an enormous shopping mecca this far out of town. The town was growing this direction, however. Subdivision after subdivision went in, many of them to accommodate JanCo's growing ranks of employees. There were a couple of other government contractors out here, too.

And every resident of the area seemed to be out in

force, shopping at the supersize grocery store, the drug-store, the craft store, the shoe store, the baby store. Every chain store known in America had opened an outlet here at Wind O' The Pines Outdoor Mall. Every restaurant was jammed, the aisles of every store packed with customers. And all of them seemed to have babies.

Rex and Craig were on foot, methodically searching each store, while Lori drove through parking lot after parking lot, scanning the parked cars for anything sus-picious, anyone who might be Denise or Lily.

There were means of escape in every direction, Rex noticed. Every street in the area converged here. Then there were alleys. A fugitive could secret himself in the back of an eighteen-wheeler and be smuggled out.

The plans Peter could have made were infinite. And he might not actually be heading here. He might have just struck out in a random direction.

"Beau, Gavin, do you still have visual contact? Over."

"We got him," Beau said. "We're staying just far enough back that he can't see us. But he's leaving a trail like a wounded elephant."

"He's bleeding?" Rex asked, surprised.

"Yeah. You must have winged him."

Somehow, Rex could take little joy from the knowl-edge that he hadn't completely missed. However, a wounded man would find it harder to run. At least he had that.

"Rex, I think I've got something." It was Lori.

"Go ahead."

"A woman sitting alone in a BMW at the KFC park-ing lot. The windows are tinted, so I can't see whether she has a baby, but she's got the driver's window cracked and she's smoking."

"What else?"

"I saw just a bit of her face when I drove past. Blond hair, sharp features. Could be called rat-faced. And one other thing. I'm not a hundred percent sure, but I thought I heard a baby crying. And she looked like she couldn't care less."

"You got a plate number?" he shot back.

"Of course." And she rattled it off.

"Craig," Rex started, but Craig interrupted.

"I'm calling in the plates now."

"Lori, keep your distance," Rex said. "I'm going to my car now. Everybody else, get ready to roll."

As soon as he approached the fast-food restaurant's parking lot, he saw the silver car. It was just sitting there. Maybe the woman's husband had gone inside to get dinner while she waited outside with the baby. But the restaurant wasn't as crowded as some of the others—it shouldn't take that long to get his order.

Rex pulled his vehicle into the drive-through line and paused in front of the menu, where he had a good view of the woman and he could study her without arousing suspicion. She looked nervous to him—and her gaze kept darting around, as if she was waiting for something.

He itched to confront her. But he decided to wait— Craig would have an answer on the plates soon.

A minute later, Craig came back on the radio. "Those plates are registered to a Nissan pickup truck."

A charged silence followed Craig's news. The BMW was almost certainly stolen.

"I can approach her based on that," Craig said. "I'm off duty, but I could still detain her if I believe she's in a stolen vehicle."

It would be a chance to let someone get close enough to verify whether Lily was inside that car. "Do it. You see Lily, signal and we'll all move in." He briefly organized how the bust would take place. A car pulled in behind him and honked; apparently he'd taken too long in making his decision about which chicken dinner to order. During his moment of distraction, the BMW roared to life.

He cursed colorfully. Had they tipped off the woman?

"Peter's broken from the woods," Gavin reported. "He's headed down the hill for the shopping center."

Sure enough, a lone man with a backpack was making his way down the slight incline, heading straight for them. He had long, stringy hair, glasses, a mustache— didn't look at all like Peter Danilov! For a split second, Rex panicked, thinking they'd made a mistake. Then he realized the clothes were the same as those Peter had been wearing at JanCo. And one side of the man's face was red with dripping blood.

Denise—for that was surely who it was—had seen Peter a few seconds before Rex had and she was already veering out of the parking lot. Rex pulled out of line and followed her. "It's definitely Denise," he said into his headset. "Don't let her get away. But don't do anything to endanger Lily." Rex was acutely conscious of the promise he'd made to Nadia, possibly the last words he would ever say to her.

He would get Lily back safe, or he would die trying.

Lori, in Beau's Mustang, had reacted more quickly than Rex and was directly behind the BMW as it pulled out into traffic. "Lori, I want you to get in front of her and be ready to cut her off. Craig?"

"I'm right behind you," Craig said. "We'll box her in."

Denise turned left at the intersection, probably intending to pull off to the shoulder as soon as possible so Peter could get in her car. Lori roared past her. Then everything happened at once. Sirens from out of nowhere. A helicopter. And a gun, pointing out the BMW's driver's window. Denise fired wildly at the Mustang, and Rex felt sick at the thought of his baby sister getting shot. But Lori skidded the car sideways like a pro and he saw her fly out, ducking behind the car with her own gun in hand.

"Hold your fire!" Rex yelled as he pulled alongside the BMW, expecting his windshield to shatter any moment. But Denise was apparently busy with other things. Moments later she jumped out the passenger side, and she had a screaming Lily held in front of her like a shield.

Obviously in a panic, her eyes wild, she squeezed off a couple of ill-aimed shots, but no one dared to shoot back when she was holding a child.

Peter joined her and grabbed Lily away from Denise, making sure the baby shielded him. Selfish bastard. He didn't care if Denise got shot. Then, with the baby propped under one arm, he held the beaker aloft as squad car after squad car screeched to a stop and officers jumped out. Some were deliberately blocking traffic, preventing innocent people from driving close to the threat.

"You all know what I can do with this, right?" Peter said. He was exhilarated by the chase, high with his own perceived power.

Apparently word of the threat had trickled down. As men in riot gear and decontamination suits gathered at the site, no one made a move toward Peter. This ridiculous show of force was Robert Candless's doing, Rex was sure. Once free of his restraints he had called in a few favors.

A man in a suit walked straight up to Rex, a bullhorn in his hand. He had curly red hair and freckles, which only clashed with the surly expression on his face, which was not at all boyish.

Lyle Palmer. Hell.

"Why," Palmer said, "do I always find the First Strike bounty hunters at the center of a big mess like this?"

Rex could have answered with a few choice words, but he didn't have time for verbal fencing with the megalomaniac detective. He kept one careful eye on Peter, Denise and Lily. "All I need is a clear shot," he said. At this distance, even with a handgun, it was child's play to hit Peter square in the head. But not while Lily was so close. He had to wait for just the right opening.

"You will not shoot," Palmer said in an urgent voice. "Do you have any idea what he's got in that bottle?"

"It's cyanide. Dangerous, but not lethal on a mass scale."

"Right," Palmer said. "Holster your gun, Bettencourt. This is a police matter now."

Rex ignored him. Peter was speaking again.

"You don't think I'll do it, do you?" he said with a

semihysterical laugh. "Or maybe you're curious to see the abomination your government dollars have produced? All I have to do is pull out the stopper and dump this on the ground, and the chain reaction will start. All your guns and tanks and aircraft carriers will be powerless to stop it." He shook the beaker for emphasis. "Or maybe you'd like to see me dump it on the kid here. Ever see a baby turn into petroleum right before your eyes? She wouldn't even be a tankful of gas."

"Peter," Denise muttered, "let's just go. Tell them to let us go."

"But this is so much fun!" Peter protested.

He was losing it. Rex saw it, and he knew that in Peter's present state of mind, he might just do the unthinkable. Rex didn't care if the idiot killed himself. But Lily was so close to him, so close to the bottle of deadly cyanide, the fumes could kill her, too.

"Denise," Rex called, "it's not too late for you. Give yourself up. Save your life."

Palmer stared in openmouthed disbelief. "What are you doing? You don't have the authority—"

"Shut up, you little weasel." It was Ace, speaking to Lyle Palmer in a deadly growl.

Denise looked as though she was about to lose it. Without warning, she dropped her gun and bolted away from Peter, directly into the arms of about a dozen cops who had her down on the ground and handcuffed before Rex could blink.

Peter was clearly shocked. "Denise!"

"Peter, give it up!" she screamed. "We can't win now."

Peter recovered himself and flashed a superior smirk,

though it was a bit frayed around the edges. "I still hold all the cards, you stupid cow." He looked at Lori. "You. Get behind the wheel of that fine automobile. You're my new chauffeur."

Lori looked to Rex for direction, and Rex nodded. *Do it,* he mouthed. It would buy him more time. All he needed was a small window of opportunity.

The baby was slipping lower down Peter's body as his attention was diverted to his audience.

"I'm going to get into that Mustang now," he announced. He held the beaker high in the air. "If anyone makes a move to stop me, if I hear a gun cock or even the sound of feet moving, I will crack this bottle onto little Lily's head." He lifted the beaker higher, almost as if he was brandishing a sword in victory. The beaker blocked his head, but he'd left a large expanse of his chest open and vulnerable.

Operating now on sheer instinct, Rex didn't hesitate. He aimed carefully and pulled the trigger. The loud report of his Glock scared everybody, but no one more than Peter. He dropped Lily, who landed with a thud on her well-padded bottom. The shock abruptly silenced her crying as she looked around, trying to figure out what was happening. Then she toppled and started rolling down the hill. She was coming right toward Rex's feet.

Rex darted in and scooped the baby up into his arms, though his gaze never left Peter.

Peter staggered back, but there was no blood, and he didn't fall. That was when Rex realized Peter was wearing a bulletproof vest.

Now Rex aimed again. He would have to go for

Peter's head this time. But Peter was faster. He uncorked the beaker, intending to make good his threat to take everyone with him. The beaker of liquid bubbled menacingly as a shocked hush fell over the crowd of cops, bounty hunters and a few curious onlookers who'd been too stupid to keep their distance.

Then Peter Danilov fell over unconscious, and the liquid spilled out over him, over the grass.

"Good God, man!" It was Robert Candless. His face was pasty white as he contemplated the end of the world. "Do you have any idea what you've just done?"

"It's cyanide," Rex said, though he knew Candless would probably have to analyze the stuff himself before he would believe that it wasn't the Petro-Nano that had just spilled all over the grass and Peter. "I tried to tell you—Nadia would not have put all of humanity at risk, not even for her daughter's sake."

"But how do you know?" Candless said in an anguished voice as he kept his gaze trained on the downed Peter Danilov, perhaps watching for signs that the voracious nanoreplicators had begun their deadly work.

"Because I know."

Chapter Fifteen

Once the dust settled, Rex was not surprised when Lyle Palmer came at him waving handcuffs and babbling about charging him with everything from interfering with a police investigation to assault to attempted murder to domestic terrorism.

"What were you thinking, hog-tying Robert Candless?" Lyle sputtered. "Do you know who that guy is, who he knows?"

"He was about to shoot an innocent woman," Rex said calmly as he cuddled Lily. The child was dirty and needed a diaper change in the worst way, but she was the sweetest thing he'd ever held in his life. He handed over his Glock, butt first, to the red-haired detective. "I'll make a deal with you, Palmer. I will turn myself in and you can charge me with whatever you want. I'll co-operate fully. But first, I'm going to deliver this child to her mother." If her mother was still alive.

"You expect me to just let you walk away with the hostage?"

"Unless you want all kinds of trouble, yes, that's exactly what you'll do. Preferably before the television crews arrive."

"He's not kidding around, Palmer." It was Ace. "Besides, you've got a couple of bona fide spies to process. Kidnappers. Russkies. Better get your licks in before the Feds get here."

Ace's advice had the desired effect on Palmer. Clearly the capture of two Russian spies was a lot more headline worthy than the arrest of a measly bounty hunter. "I'll expect to see you at headquarters first thing tomorrow morning," Palmer said to Rex. "If you don't show, I'll find you."

In his dreams. If Rex wanted to disappear, he could. "I'll be there bright and early," Rex replied. With his lawyer.

"He can't make anything stick," Ace said after Lyle Palmer had walked away. "If anything, you'll be called a hero for tracking down and shooting a spy." He nodded toward Peter's inert form. A HazMat team, complete with a full complement of decontamination equipment, was preparing to approach the body. "Looks like he's dead. What was in the bottle again?"

"Cyanide." Rex was starting to feel like a broken record. "The concentrated fumes are instantly lethal. That's why I pulled the trigger. He was threatening to open the bottle with Lily right there. It wouldn't have started an ecological disaster, but it might have killed Nadia's baby."

"She looks okay." Ace smiled at Lily and tickled her tummy with one finger. She hid her face against Rex's chest.

"I'd like to have a picture of that," said Lori as she sauntered over. "I think she likes you."

Lord knew why. He usually scared pets and small

children. But the fact that Lily was clinging to him, cooing and gurgling, had the most amazing effect on him.

"Why are you standing around?" Lori asked. "Shouldn't you be at the hospital?"

"Have you heard something?" Rex asked anxiously.

"I've been on the phone. She's in surgery, that's all I know. Might be a good idea if you were there when she woke up."

"Thanks, sis. You did great tonight, by the way. You can be a member of my team anytime."

"I told you she was ready," Ace said.

Lori beamed, then proved herself useful one more time by coming up with a baby car seat for Lily and installing it in the back seat of Rex's Blazer. "I took it from the BMW," she whispered. "Shh."

"OUCH." THAT WAS the first word Nadia was conscious of as she emerged from a gray fog of anesthetic. It was followed by a more insistent, "Ouch!" And she realized she was the one speaking.

It felt as though someone had stuck a knife into her ribs. She cracked her eyes open, but the white-hot light that tried to enter her brain was too intense, so she closed them again.

Peter. Peter had shot her! Panic seized her and she tried to sit up, but a firm hand pushed her back down onto a soft bed. Not cold concrete, but soft, crisp sheets and a pillow for her aching head. She had to get up, though. She had to find Lily.

"Don't try to move," came the low, soothing voice. "You've just come out of surgery."

"Then someone *did* stick a knife between my ribs," she mumbled as she began putting it all together. She was in a hospital. Now she remembered doctors and nurses swarming around her, a ride in an ambulance.

She tried again to open her eyes, this time succeeding. And as the blurry world around her spun and tried to right itself, she saw a face hovering over hers. "Rex?"

"I'm here, sweetheart."

"What happened? Where's Lily?"

Rex's face disappeared for a moment, and Nadia tried to turn her head, but her body parts weren't cooperating. Then Lily was there, reaching for her with a big smile. "Mama!" she shrieked, and Nadia hugged her with the one arm that wasn't attached to an IV. She sobbed with relief and joy. Her baby was safe. She was wearing strange clothes that didn't fit, but she smelled sweet and clean. Someone had bathed her and given her a fresh diaper.

Rex just stood there, supporting Lily so her full weight didn't fall on Nadia's incision, and mother and daughter hugged each other for a long, long time as tears coursed down Nadia's cheeks. She'd been so afraid this moment would never come. Then Lily wiggled, and Nadia realized she was hugging her daughter too hard and eased up.

Rex pulled her back up into his arms, looking remarkably at ease. "Your mama needs to rest, okay, Lily?"

"Rex, you sing me?"

"I'll sing you in a little while," Rex said. "I have to talk to your mama."

"You've been singing to her?" Nadia asked, trying to picture the rough-and-tumble bounty hunter singing *The Itsy Bitsy Spider* or *Farmer in the Dell*.

He shrugged. "She likes Jimi Hendrix."

Coming a bit more awake, Nadia saw that she was in a cubicle with curtained partitions. A recovery room, she guessed. One of the curtains wiggled, then a hand pushed it aside. Lori stuck her head in. "Is she awake yet?"

"Come in, Lori," Nadia said, and Lori entered with a big grin.

"You had us scared," Lori said, perching on the end of the bed. "How do you feel?"

"Fine, now that Lily is back." To be honest, she was in a whole lot of physical pain, worse as the minutes ticked by and the anesthetic wore off. But she wasn't going to mention it. She would endure ten times that amount of pain if she could just hold Lily again.

"Have you told her?" Lori asked Rex.

He rolled his eyes. "She just woke up two minutes ago," Rex said. "Give me half a chance."

"Told me what?" Nadia asked. "Is Lily okay?"

"Lily's fine," Rex assured her. "We had a doctor check her out. Lori, could you take the baby for a few minutes? I need some time alone with Nadia."

"Sure."

Nadia wanted to object. She'd only just been reunited with Lily. She didn't want to be separated from her ever, ever again. But Rex took her hand and squeezed it. "Just for a few minutes. Then she'll be back."

Seeing the gravity in Rex's eyes, Nadia bit her tongue and let Lori take her baby away.

"What is it?" she asked Rex when they were alone.

"It's Peter. He's dead."

"Oh." She refrained from adding, *Is that all?* But

frankly, she felt only relief at the knowledge that her ex-husband was dead. She would never have to fear him again. Lily would never know him, and that was for the best. "How did it happen? How did you catch him?"

He told her a long and complex story of cut fuel lines and a chase through the woods, a stolen BMW and a standoff at the side of a rural highway and something about KFC, but her mind wasn't processing at full speed.

"When I saw an opening, I shot him," Rex said. "I wanted him to let go of Lily."

"I guess that answers the question of whether you can fire your gun."

"Yes, I guess it does. But that's not what killed him. He was wearing a bulletproof vest. But my shot knocked him over, and he did let go of Lily. She rolled down the hill practically into my arms, which was a good thing. Because he opened the beaker he took from you."

"Oh, my God." Nadia wasn't shocked so much by what had happened as by what *could* have happened if she had given in to Peter's demands. She had hoped he wasn't crazy enough to initiate an ecological disaster, but clearly he had been. "So is that what killed him? The hydrochloric acid?"

"With amazing efficiency."

"Then I'm the one who caused his death, technically." She smiled. "Good." She hadn't forgotten that Peter had threatened to cut off her baby's fingers, and she felt no remorse over his death. "Is everyone else okay? I can't believe your whole team risked their lives for me, for Lily."

He shrugged. "It's what we do."

"And you'll be paid handsomely, too. I don't even remember what fee we agreed on—that seems like a life-time ago. But I'll triple it."

"You can pay the others for their part," he said. "But you don't have to pay me."

"Why shouldn't I?"

He started to respond, but Lori entered the cubicle again with Lily on her hip. Lily spotted Rex and held out her arms to him. "Rex!"

"I think you've made a fan," Nadia observed.

"Sorry," Lori whispered. "I know you wanted me gone longer, but I'm hiding from reporters. They're everywhere, and they're not buying the load of bull Lyle Palmer and that guy from JanCo are trying to pass off as the truth."

"Palmer is taking credit for everything, I assume?" Rex asked.

"Well, Lyle is trying to take credit for breaking up an international spy ring. Craig told me Denise is talking, trying to save her own skin. They've made some more arrests—Vlad Popolov is in custody. And they've raided the Payton Gun Club and found an arsenal of weapons that made the Branch Davidians look like kids with popguns. Apparently Popolov owned that, too. He's convinced America is on the brink of revolution and anarchy. We're not sure of Andy Arquette's role—he may just be a gun-happy nut on Peter's payroll."

"What is Candless saying?" Nadia asked, concerned about the security breach she had caused.

"Oh, Candless is putting a completely different spin on things. He denies that JanCo Labs is producing anything hazardous. He's passing Peter off as a disgruntled employee who went berserk."

Rex grinned. "Let's hope they keep chasing each other's tails and forget all about me."

"We should get out of here while we have the chance," Lori said to her brother. "I know how you hate publicity."

Rex just grinned. "I can take the heat. Besides, someone has to take care of Lily until Nadia is stronger. You go on, though. Save yourself."

Lori looked at Rex as if he was a bit addled in the brains. "Thanks, I will." And she disappeared.

"You don't have to stick around just to baby-sit Lily," Nadia said. "I'm sure someone else would do it—a volunteer, or—"

"Hush. I'm happy to be here. Besides, don't you want to know why you don't have to pay my fee?"

"Yes, as a matter of fact."

"Because I'm giving you the family discount."

She didn't really get what he meant, but she was too tired to figure it out. She drifted back to sleep.

REX WATCHED HER SLEEP, alert to any change in her breathing, any sign that she might be having difficulty. But her surgeon had said she came through the operation beautifully, that he'd been able to remove the bullet and repair the damage to her lung. She'd lost a fair amount of blood and had gone into mild shock, but they'd been able to stop the bleeding quickly once medical personnel had arrived. She'd been stable going into surgery, and her vital signs had remained strong all during the procedure and after. Her doctors had assured him she would survive, barring unforeseen circumstances.

Rex was on guard, just in case an unforeseen circumstance tried to sneak its way past him.

While she slept, they moved her to a room. Nurses and volunteers stopped by on a regular basis to check on her—and to sneak peeks at the woman who'd been shot by a Russian spy and the child who'd been kidnapped by one. Rumors were flying all over the hospital, all over the city, but so far the press had been kept away from him and Nadia.

When she awoke again a couple of hours later, she seemed more alert. She refused pain medication, claimed she didn't need it, though he could tell by the tightness around her mouth that she wasn't entirely comfortable.

"I thought you'd be in Tahiti by now," she said.

"I'll get there." He'd had that fantasy again, the one where he lay on the beach while a bikini-clad woman rubbed him with suntan oil. Only the woman had a face now.

"Will you explain again why I can't pay you?" Now sitting up in bed, she was able to hold Lily on her lap. Lily, who was exhausted from her ordeal, seemed content to doze there in her mother's arms. Strictly speaking, she shouldn't have even been allowed to visit. But Rex wasn't about to let anyone separate Nadia from her baby, and no one dared cross him. "You said something about a family discount, but last time I checked, we weren't related."

"We could fix that," Rex said.

Nadia blinked a couple of times. "Are you saying…"

"I'm saying I want to marry you."

"But—"

"I'll give you time to think about it. But, honestly, you're the first woman I ever met who was strong enough to put up with me. The first one who wasn't scared of me. The first one to trust me."

"You're an honorable man," Nadia said. "Why wouldn't anyone trust you?"

"Maybe you see something others don't," he said. "That's why I'm not going to walk away from you without a fight. It's…it's why I love you."

She stared at him a few moments, speechless, as her eyes swam with unshed tears. She seemed on the brink of admitting something, then abruptly broke eye contact. "Well, Lily likes you." She sounded a bit breathless.

"I like her, too. In fact, I'm feeling remarkably territorial about her. Every nurse in this whole hospital has volunteered to baby-sit, but I've told them all no. *I* want to take care of her. And what's the big deal about changing diapers? I can do it in thirty seconds flat."

Nadia's jaw dropped.

"I know this has come out of left field, and you don't have to answer right away. Just think about it."

"I don't have to," she said. "I do love you, Rex. But I love Lily, too, and look what happened to her. The ones I care about will always be in danger from people who might want to manipulate me—"

"Do you honestly think that scares me? Anyway, it's all the more reason to have me around. Who would dare try to wrangle secrets from you with me on watch?"

"That is a good point." He watched her face as she

mulled over the possibilities. She didn't reveal much. Even her tears didn't tell him much. Tears of joy? Regret? Was she just overwhelmed with everything?

Not content to merely watch, he came closer and brushed her tears away with his hand. "Only one thing truly scares me," he said softly, "and that's the idea of living the rest of my life without love. Without you."

Nadia blinked, and he realized she was getting sleepy again. She was still suffering from the aftereffects of anesthesia, and he felt guilty for confronting her at a time like this with his declarations of love and a marriage proposal out of nowhere.

"Sweetheart, forget I said anything," he said gently. "You just focus on getting well. We'll talk another time."

"You know," she said drowsily, "when I was a girl I used to dream about discovering a cure for cancer." And with that startling non sequitur, she fell asleep again.

Rex pondered her words for a full thirty seconds before he realized that she had, indeed, accepted his proposal.

THEY WERE MARRIED two months later, just as spring flowers were starting to bloom, in the same rose garden where Beau and his wife, Aubrey, had married the previous year. Lily was too young to be a flower girl, but they let her be one anyway, and she spent most of the wedding trying to eat the rose petals in her basket.

Nadia had healed quickly from her wound, and other than a twinge every now and then when she twisted the wrong way, she felt better than ever. When she returned to work, she immediately requested a transfer to a different sector at JanCo. She was still in nanotechnology, but now she was working on pharmaceutical applications—in particular, a nanodevice that would deliver drugs specifically targeted to cancer cells while leaving normal tissue unaffected. It was the most exciting work she'd ever done, and no foreign governments or terrorists were the slightest bit interested.

Rex was still a bounty hunter, still working for First Strike, but he had scaled back his travel. No more tracking fugitives all over the country for weeks at a time. He didn't need those more exciting cases to keep his blood pumping or remind him he was alive. He didn't need to punish himself by pushing himself to the limits of physical endurance. He had found his peace, and he had all the excitement he needed with learning how to be a husband and father.

Lily did not seem to suffer from the ordeal at all. After she caught up on her sleep and food, she regained her former sunny disposition.

When it came time for a toast at the wedding reception, held in a gazebo festooned with so many flowers it was about to collapse, no one knew quite what to say. Ace, who was seldom short on words, took a stab at being humorous.

"To Rex and Nadia, the cutest couple I ever saw. I mean, look, she practically has to stand on a box to kiss him."

Lori jabbed Ace in the ribs with her elbow.

"Well," Ace said, "you try it. Making a wedding toast is tricky business."

Rex sent Ace a nod of appreciation for trying. Then he picked Nadia up and set her on a bench, so he had to look up to her. He held his glass high. "To Nadia, who is not only the most beautiful woman in the world, but the strongest I've ever known." And he truly meant that. He hadn't known exactly how strong until, a day after Peter's death, someone had discovered Nadia's suicide note. Until then, he hadn't known she'd planned to end her own life to save her daughter's, and his love for her had swelled to even greater proportions.

The crowd of wedding guests grew utterly silent, and the smart-ass toasts were forgotten as everyone could literally feel the love coursing between bride and groom. Married couples intertwined their fingers, remembering how it was to be transformed by love, and those who hadn't yet experienced it were awed, silently vowing never to settle for less.

* * * * *

Don't miss Kara Lennox's new miniseries,
BLOND JUSTICE, *featuring*
three jilted blondes and the man who
conned them all, only from
Harlequin American Romance!

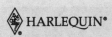

eHARLEQUIN.com

The Ultimate Destination for Women's Fiction

For **FREE online reading,** visit
www.eHarlequin.com now and enjoy:

Online Reads
Read **Daily** and **Weekly** chapters from
our Internet-exclusive stories by your
favorite authors.

Interactive Novels
Cast your vote to help decide how these
stories unfold...then stay tuned!

Quick Reads
For shorter romantic reads, try our
collection of Poems, Toasts, & More!

Online Read Library
Miss one of our online reads?
Come here to catch up!

Reading Groups
Discuss, share and rave with other
community members!

For great reading online, visit www.eHarlequin.com today!

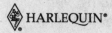

If you enjoyed what you just read,
then we've got an offer you can't resist!

Take 2 bestselling
love stories FREE!
Plus get a FREE surprise gift!

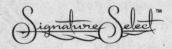

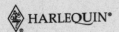

N™xt

Coming this July from NEXT™

Sometimes a woman has to make her own luck.
Find out how Kasey does exactly that!

LUCKY by Jennifer Greene

**Don't miss the moving new novel by *USA TODAY*
bestselling author Jennifer Greene.**